Every Witch Way but Brewed

Magical Misfits Mysteries - book 14

K.E. O'Connor

K.E. O'Connor Books

EVERY WITCH WAY BUT BREWED

Copyright © 2024 by K.E. O'Connor

ISBN: 978-1-915378-81-1

Written by: K.E. O'Connor

Edited by Lana Mowdry

Cover Design by Victoria Cooper

Chapter 1

High drama

"That striped hummingbird with the serrated talons was something else." My wonderful witch, Zandra Crypt, strolled along the main street in Crimson Cove. She was inspecting a ragged tear in the sleeve of her favorite leather jacket.

"Be grateful for your protective outerwear," I said. "The winged beast would have torn through your arm if it had gotten a hold. It wanted to."

"I wear this jacket because it's cool rather than for protection, but I see your point." Zandra rolled her shoulders and yawned loudly. "I keep waiting for things to calm down at work, but ever since the whole weird pizza incident, everything feels unsettled. Don't you think?"

"I don't think. I know." I twitched my booping snooter. We'd been putting in extra hours for weeks to keep up with the additional work our harassed boss, Barney Hoffman, kept throwing at us. Every morning, we'd arrive at animal control, and there'd be another disaster to deal with that had exploded overnight. Despite extensive investigations to find the source of this continued chaos, we were stumped. Crimson Cove appeared to be festering with anger and malicious deeds, and it was only growing.

"We deserve a treat after our hard work," I said. "Let's stop by Sorcha's café. The dinner rush should be over, and you've barely spent any time together recently."

"We've both been too busy working to hang out," Zandra said. "Sorcha hasn't even been by Vorana's for breakfast in a while."

"It could be another distraction that's keeping her away. Her relationship with Denver is going nicely. He's such a sweet vampire."

"Most likely," Zandra said. "I'll message Vorana, see if she wants to join us for dinner. She'll appreciate a night off from cooking for us."

While Zandra tapped out a message, I trotted ahead, my stomach encouraging me to hurry. All this work, rounding up critters that misbehave and teaching their owners how to look after them properly, made me starving. I'd had three breakfasts, my own lunch and half of Zandra's, and a snack mid-afternoon, yet my belly growled like a hungry bear fresh out of her hibernation cave.

Zandra caught up with me as she pocketed her mobile snow globe. "I assume you'll have something featuring smoked salmon."

"I'm a creature of habit. It's nothing to be ashamed of," I said.

"I don't know whether to go for a burger or a big bowl of gooey pasta. I'm in need of stodge." Zandra reached for the door to the café and pulled it open.

A large cake flew out, smacking her squarely on the forehead.

She yelped and stumbled back as the cake slid down her face and dropped to the ground. A second cake swirled through the air and whacked her in the chest, making a loud wet thwap.

"Hey! Whoever's tossing cake at me, you need to stop." Zandra swiped cream off her black T-shirt, smearing a slug-like stain all the way to the waistband of her jeans.

I peeked around the corner of the doorway. Sorcha Creer had a cake in hand and was ready to let it fly. "Stop! We come in peace. No more cake missiles."

Sorcha's expression shifted from angered frustration to shock, and she lowered her arm. "Juno! Oh my goddess. I'm sorry! I got so angry I ended up taking it out on the cakes. You weren't supposed to be standing there."

"What did the cake do to you?" Zandra was still swiping cream off her forehead as she stepped into the café.

I helpfully hopped onto her shoulder and licked sticky cream off her face with my wonderfully raspy tongue. It was an effective cleaning tool.

"It's not the cakes. Look at this place!" Sorcha gestured around the empty café, her bright ginger curls a halo around her freckled face. "There isn't a single person in here."

"We hoped we'd missed the dinner rush," I said.

"Missed it! It swept past without the door opening once." Sorcha slapped the cake onto a tray.

"Have we missed something?" I asked. "Is there an event in town that everyone's attending instead of coming here?"

"I suppose you could call it that. I'm finished. Ruined. All of these cakes will have to be thrown out." Sorcha jabbed a finger at the almost full display cabinet of delicious treats.

"I don't understand." Zandra grabbed a clean towel from behind the counter and scrubbed at her shirt. "Did you over order?"

"I ordered the same as I always do," Sorcha said. "And I made the same amount of cakes, baked the same amount of potatoes, and filled the same amount of sandwiches. No one is coming to my café anymore. I've even been opening earlier and shutting later in the hope of catching more people, but they don't come."

"Have you received a bad food hygiene rating?" I lifted my head. There was a curious scent of hot, furry bodies in the air.

"I have the highest rating." Sorcha grimaced at her sticky hand. "But I haven't had a single customer all day. What am I supposed to do with all this food?"

"We'll take it," I said, still looking around, attempting to locate the source of the curious smell. Could that be what was putting people off? It was pungent.

"That's too much for us to handle," Zandra said. "But we're customers. Here for dinner."

"After hitting you with cake, I should feed you for free." Sorcha's bottom lip jutted out. "I really am sorry. I don't know what came over me."

"Since we're your only customers, we'll pay. But what gives? Why is nobody coming in for food?" Zandra headed to the counter and glanced at the chalkboard menu.

"Why do you think?" Sorcha's tone was full of bitterness as she stamped over. "Loyalty in this town is dead."

"Is that so?" Zandra glanced at me, her eyebrows raised.

While I half-listened to Sorcha rant about the lack of loyalty these days, I finally located the curious scent. Although, in doing so, I almost got a nasty gash on the end of my booping snooter. Tucked into a corner of the café, right at the back, was a box with three spitting kittens inside. They were delightfully fluffy, black, with amber eyes, their tiny needle claws extended as they attempted to defend themselves.

"Oh! Be careful of them." Sorcha noticed me investigating the café's new residents. "Someone dumped them on the doorstep. They must know I'm a soft touch for waifs and strays. And with Finn still away, they figured the animal sanctuary isn't taking in any creatures."

"These kittens have magic." I kept a safe distance from the box, since the furious bundles of adorable fluffiness sparked with power. Power that felt a little too big for such tiny paws to control.

"I wonder if that's why they were ditched," Sorcha said. "Whoever owned them didn't realize what they were taking on. Those kittens may be tiny, but that little one at the back with the piece missing out of his ear set fire to a tablecloth."

"Could they be the reason customers are staying away?" Zandra pointed out what she wanted from the menu. "They don't want to be chargrilled when they grab their tuna melts and cappuccinos."

"I haven't had the kittens in here all day." Sorcha strode behind the counter. "But I figured, since no one was coming in, there'd be no harm in keeping a closer eye on my three bundles of fury. They never seem to sleep, constantly need feeding, and are always angry. They're also super cute, though. All I want to do is cuddle them."

I stared at the cute fluffies with focused interest. It had been a long time since I'd encountered such small creatures with so much contained energy. It must be over a hundred years. Possibly longer. I was intrigued as to where they'd come from and what their source of power was. Since they were so small, they wouldn't be able to tell me. All they'd want at the moment was lots of food, play, and hours of sleep. Growing kittens burned through energy.

"Smoked salmon?" Sorcha asked me.

"As always." I risked a sniff of the kittens then returned to the counter, where Zandra lounged as Sorcha got to work on making our food. "You were talking about lack of loyalty. Who's being disloyal to you?"

"My problems are thanks to Verity Yummy and her gross scones and sneery smile," Sorcha said.

"I know that name," Zandra said. "Where from?"

"Verity runs the new tearoom." I glanced back at the kittens. "Do you think your customers are purchasing their treats from her, rather than buying from you?"

Sorcha thumped down a knife. "I know they are. I shut for twenty minutes this afternoon and went snooping. The stupid tearoom was packed. I can't figure out why. To start with, the name is ridiculous. *The English Tea Shoppe*. Two p's and one e. What affected nonsense. How do you even say that? Shoppie?"

"It is twee," I said. "Verity must be hoping to evoke an old-fashioned English charm."

Sorcha grunted. "The food looks fake. And Verity is the worst. I stood on the other side of the street and watched her interacting with customers. She's so fake-friendly, all smiles and over-the-top laughter. It's disgusting."

"I hate it when people are nice," Zandra said.

"That's just it! There wasn't a genuine ounce of niceness about anything Verity did," Sorcha said. "And she gave away free food to every customer. She handed them a bag of goodies as they left the café. Awful."

"That's why they keep going back," Zandra said. "I'm a sucker for a free cake, although I prefer it when they're not slung at my head."

"Verity must be drugging them. Or bewitching them. It's unnatural behavior. How can she turn a profit by giving away stuff?" Sorcha placed a plate of smoked salmon in front of me. "She's been open less than a month, and since then, my customer base has dwindled to nothing. Today was the end of times for my café. If I have no one to serve, I'll make no money. I'll have to shut. And then what will I do?"

A small hot bundle of hissing anger and needle claws landed on my back. I tensed, but I'd heard the small kitten approach and had readied myself for the impact.

"Behave yourself, little one," I murmured. "Or it'll be back in the box with your siblings."

The kitten hissed fiercely in my ear, but its tiny body trembled. It may be furious, but it was full of fear. A second later, the adorable little monster was joined by a sibling, and I ended up with two hissing bundles of anger and fluff riding on my back as I showed them the full extent of the café, letting my hunger marinate as the tasty scent of smoked fish tempted me.

Zandra watched with amusement as she tucked into her food. "Your customers will come back. It's a new tea room, so everyone will want to take a look."

"No one wants an overpriced tearoom in Crimson Cove," Sorcha said. "Why would they, when they have my place? I know everyone's order. And I'm fast on my feet. People never have to wait more than fifteen minutes for their food."

"Verity only took ten minutes to serve us." Zandra's fork froze halfway to her mouth.

"Serve you! Unless you want another cake in the face, you won't eat there ever again." Sorcha scowled fiercely. "Please tell me your lunch was disgusting. Bland? Under-cooked? No, worse, overcooked? An inedible pile of nasty mush."

"It was... I don't remember." Zandra stuffed a huge mouthful of food into her mouth and chewed furiously to avoid answering the question.

I finished my turn around the room with the kittens. The tearoom offerings had been incredible, but I wasn't brave enough to tell Sorcha, given the mood she was in.

Sorcha groaned and tipped her head back to stare at the ceiling. "Verity's scones didn't look terrible. That's what she's selling. Old English charm. She's even faking a British accent. It grated on my ears."

"There were a lot of people there having a fancy early afternoon tea," Zandra said. "Verity kept bringing out towers of food. There were little sandwiches cut into triangles, a tray with loads of small cakes, and then a tray full of scones with jam and cream."

I hurried over, the two kittens still attached to me as I saw Sorcha's face shift back to rage. "It's a novelty. Once people have been to the *English Tea Shoppe* a few times, they'll get bored with the scones and cream and come back here."

Sorcha's bottom lip poked out. "They'd better. I can't go on much longer if my customers don't come back. I should do some deals. Offer discounted dining. A free goodie bag of cake with every order?"

"Don't undersell yourself," I said. "Your food is excellent, and your company is even better. People will miss you. They'll return, and everything will go back to normal."

The café door opened, and a tall, willowy woman with long silver hair down to her waist, wearing a boho dress that brushed across the floor, entered. She looked around, a huge smile on her face. As she drew closer, she smelled of brewed tea and some kind of flower. It wasn't an unappealing scent.

Sorcha's expression brightened at the prospect of another customer. "What can I get you? Everything on the menu is available."

"What a wonderful little place," the woman said. "Sadly, it's not the café I'm looking for. Have either of you heard of *The English Tea Shoppe*? It only opened recently."

Sorcha's smile faded. "Perhaps. What do you want with that place?"

"The owner is planning an event for the local community. I'm a tea leaf diviner and will be holding sessions so visitors can have their fortune read. Could you point me in the right direction?"

Sorcha grimaced. "Are you sure I can't get you anything to eat? I have a five-star rating on my sausage rolls."

"No, thank you. Verity promised me dinner. I'm looking forward to it. Her 'queen of the cream teas' offer is a once-in-a-lifetime experience."

"I can imagine," Sorcha grumbled. "Out of here, turn left, and walk for five minutes. It's on the right-hand side. There's cheap looking pink and yellow bunting outside, so you can't miss it."

"Thank you. Blessings be with you both." The woman turned and drifted out of the café, leaving behind a sour mood that emanated from Sorcha.

"Did you hear that?" Sorcha grabbed a cookie and savaged it with her teeth. "Verity is manipulating everyone by holding some ridiculous community event. Can't the locals see she's using them? She's plying them with treats and stupid fun just so she can take their money."

"A community event involving cream teas and tea leaf reading sounds dreadful," I murmured.

Zandra shook her head at me, a gentle warning to tread carefully around such a surly Sorcha. "Juno, come and eat your smoked salmon. And put those kittens down before they set fire to your fur. The one at the back is smoking."

"If I could put them down, I would, but they've embedded their claws into my fur. We shall have to adopt them." I occasionally had a maternal urge, and I felt it now with these adorable babies clinging to me.

"There's no room in the basement for feisty kittens that enjoy fire starting," Zandra said. "Put them back and don't even think about sneaking them home. I'll know if you do."

It was tempting to argue the point, but I had a lot on, and taking on the demands of powerfully magical kittens of unknown origin was a task for another week. As I was heading back to the kittens' cardboard home, the café door opened again. Vorana Stowell walked in, a pile of books under one arm and a brown paper bag in her other hand.

She smiled when she saw Sorcha and Zandra. "I'm glad you're both here. As I was passing that fabulous new tea room, Verity came out and gave me these scones to sample. What do you think? Scones and jam for dinner? There's even a pot of cream."

Sorcha groaned. "Shall I put the closed for good sign in the window now?"

Chapter 2

Spy mission

Vorana poured Zandra a coffee and made herself one before sitting at the breakfast table in her airy, bright kitchen. "I spent all night thinking about what an idiot I was. I really put my foot in it with Sorcha, but I didn't know she felt so strongly about the new teashop."

"You're not the only one who messed up." I tried a piece of egg Vorana had lightly poached for me. "Zandra let slip we'd been to the teashop for lunch recently and how fast the service was."

"It's because of the house-elves," Zandra said. "They live to serve, and Verity has a troop of them working in her café. They were running around non-stop, although you barely noticed them. We placed our order, and it just appeared."

"There is something magical about that place." I glanced at Sage's plate. She was chewing her way through a piece of bacon. She growled a warning at me not to even think about taking it from her. As if I'd do such a thing to my irascible feline friend.

"Everybody loves Sorcha's café." Vorana reached for a scone, a scone left over from Verity's delicious offerings. "She serves good, traditional food. She's always dependable. The teashop is a luxury. People won't go there every day."

"The cakes were amazing, though." Zandra helped herself to a scone and smothered it in preserves.

Vorana nodded enthusiastically. "Yes! And I don't even like black tea, but I couldn't get enough of what was being poured. Verity asked me about my favorite flavors, disappeared for a few minutes, and came back with a huge teapot that she'd brewed specifically to meet my needs. I was unsure, but when I took a sip, it was perfect. I drank the entire pot of tea."

"She was running to the bathroom every five minutes because of it," Sage muttered.

"You don't like the teashop?" I asked Sage.

"I prefer savory. The cakes looked fine, and everyone else loved them. I tried a dollop of cream. It was delicious. Not as good as this bacon, though."

"We should investigate at lunchtime," Zandra said, "to make sure Verity isn't bewitching everyone and turning them against Sorcha. She was so upset her customers have vanished."

"Are you sure you don't want to go so you can investigate more of the delicious cake?" I asked.

Zandra bit into a scone and shrugged. "There's always room for more cake. And hopefully, Verity won't throw scones at me."

"I've never seen Sorcha so angry," Vorana said. "I thought she was going to toss me out of the café when I showed up with—what did she call them—traitorous scones made by the hand of a she-beast?"

"Traitorous *treats* made by the hand of a she-beast. You arrived at the worst possible moment," I said. "But Sorcha will forgive us in a day or two. We'll make an extra effort to go to the café and buy lots of food." It would also give me a chance to spend more time with those cute kittens.

"Not this lunchtime," Zandra said. "Let's do some undercover work. Make sure there's nothing suspicious about Verity and her delicious scones."

Vorana clinked her mug against Zandra's. "It's a date."

After a busy morning of dealing with more mischievous creatures, we were heading away from animal control for a well-earned break and some much needed food.

Randal Nix, Zandra's object of affection, although she'd never admit it, strolled around the corner of the building. He wore a large metal helmet, spirals shooting out of it in different directions, wobbling in the breeze.

"Greetings! That's a new look for you." I resisted the urge to leap on his shoulder and bat a quivering spiral.

He adjusted the helmet as it almost slid down over his eyes and grinned at us. "I've been out all morning, testing those strange signals. Ever since I picked up the readings when you were investigating the vampire staking, I've taken daily recordings to make sure nothing's out of kilter."

"The readings are still strange?" Zandra asked.

"Stranger than ever. Take a look at this." He lifted a small handheld gadget with a green screen that had a number of wiggly lines running across it. "See those spikes? They're happening at regular intervals. Then, there's a massive spike, but it vanishes as quickly as it shows up. I've tested the magic wards around the entire town. They're all functioning normally, so it's not them glitching."

"What is causing it?" I asked. Spikes of magic suggested an instability lurking within town. Unstable magic was never enjoyable to be around.

"So far, I'm puzzled as to their origin. I've been going into the forest and testing the ley lines to see if the magic is unsettled, but it's not coming from there." Randal peered at the screen.

"Could it be someone living in Crimson Cove manipulating magic?" I asked. "The town is known for its powerful magic users. They congregate here. And sometimes, they aren't always on their best behavior."

"Like attracts like," Zandra said. "Maybe the weird readings are from your malfunctioning equipment."

Randal's forehead crinkled. "Um... I don't think so. I checked it just yesterday."

Zandra shrugged. "We're going to get scones."

"Oh! You're visiting *The English Tea Shoppe*?" Randal's grin reappeared. "I've been in every day. Sometimes, I grab lunch and dinner from there. I don't know what Verity puts in her food, but I can't get enough of it."

"Make an effort and visit Sorcha's café today," I said. "She's had barely any customers since the teashop opened. She's feeling unloved."

Randal frowned. "I guess I could. It's been a while since I've had a sausage roll. But whenever I get hungry, I just think about Verity's cakes. And she's super nice, too. She gave me a free bag of misshapen scones. She said they weren't pretty enough to sell, but she hates food to go to waste. I don't care what they look like. They tasted amazing."

Zandra's eyes narrowed. "We'd invite you along, but this is an undercover operation. We want to make sure Verity isn't doing anything dodgy to her food."

"What kind of dodgy are you talking about?" Randal asked. "I could tag along and take readings, just to be sure. She also said she wanted to see my latest experiment, so I'm sure she won't mind."

"What would you be taking readings of?" I asked.

"I'm not sure. Interference? Weird magic vibes? I won't know until I see it on the screen." Randal held up his device.

"You're good," Zandra said. "We're meeting Vorana on her lunch break."

"Sure, sure. I get it. Dumb idea. I don't want to be a third wheel."

"You'd be a fourth wheel, since I'll be there too," I said. "And if Sage joins us, there'll be five wheels."

"Um, sure. That sounds busy. Lots of wheels." Randal let out a gentle sigh.

"Another time." I hated to see that sad, abandoned puppy dog look on Randal's face whenever Zandra rejected him. I knew she liked him and only kept him at arm's length because she was terrified of commitment and hopelessly inexperienced with adult relationships. I needed to knock sense into these two and get them together before the lovely Verity and her yummy scones swooped in and took Randal away.

"I need to check these readings anyway," Randal said. "And you're right. I'll go to Sorcha's café and make sure she knows how much I appreciate her food. Although perhaps I'll stop at the teashop on my way back and grab dessert."

"Sounds like a plan," Zandra said. "See you later."

I murmured a goodbye to Randal and hurried after Zandra, who was striding away. I briefly considered chiding her for her inability to inject any form of romance into her friendship with Randal, but it would fall on blocked ears. My witch was as stubborn as she was perfect.

We stopped outside the attractively painted cream building with bunting fluttering lightly in the breeze.

"The place is packed," Zandra muttered. "I hope we can get a table."

"I see Vorana inside," I said. "She's got spare seats."

"Then what are we waiting for?" Zandra shoved open the door, and an alluring scent of freshly baked bread, warm sweet scones, and perfectly brewed tea drifted out to greet us. A few seconds later, a house-elf who came up to Zandra's waist, wearing a smart butler's outfit, approached us. We explained who we were with, and he obediently took us to Vorana. Sage sat on her lap, out of her harness, her front paws resting on the table.

"I'm glad you're here," Vorana said as we settled into seats. "People have been eyeballing these chairs like they're priceless works of art. The house-elves have been turning customers away."

I looked around the pleasantly scented café. It was immaculately painted in soft shades of white and cream. The wooden tables were covered in clean white linen cloths, and everyone was drinking tea from fine china cups with matching saucers. Behind the counter, several house-elves moved at lightning speed, filling plates with tiny cakes and pouring tea.

While we browsed the menu, I noticed several towers of miniature cakes brought out, enveloped in the delighted oohs and aahs of hungry customers waiting to taste the delicacies.

"I really want a deluxe platter," Vorana said. "I've watched the food come out, and most people are ordering that. It has everything. Sandwiches, cakes, and those perfect scones."

"And you get free unlimited tea refills." A house-elf appeared beside our table, a notepad and pencil in hand, ready to take our order. "I thoroughly recommend the deluxe afternoon tea platter. We serve it all day. You can even have it for breakfast. Many people do."

"Does it have sweet and savory?" Vorana asked.

The house-elf nodded. "If you don't like it, we guarantee you get to eat for free and your money back."

"You can't ask for better than that," Vorana said. "What do you say? We could get two deluxe platters and share the meat and fish with Sage and Juno."

"Familiars get their own plate," the house-elf said. "They can choose meat, cheese, fish, or sweet."

"That sounds divine," I said. "Fish for me."

"How chewy is the meat?" Sage asked. "I've not got many teeth."

"We will warm it and cut it into tiny pieces if that would be your preference," the house-elf said. "We boil it lightly in bone broth, so it's extra tender. Barely any chewing required."

"That doesn't sound terrible," Sage said. "Put me down for a meat plate."

Once the house-elf had taken our order, he vanished as quickly as he'd appeared. Before we had a chance to speak, napkins were draped in laps, warm cups and saucers delivered, and a large freshly brewed pot of tea appeared in a beautiful flower-patterned teapot.

Vorana looked around the café with wonder in her eyes. "I feel like I'm being spoiled."

"You're not the only one." I focused on the other customers. Barney and Ember sat at a table with Tia and Binky from the bakery. Cythera and Maverick from Angel Force had a small table at the back, although Cythera was facing the wall and hadn't seen us come in. I even spotted Roland Moldsworth and his curious familiar, Nimbus, at a table, a half-finished platter of scones in front of them, and Roland feeding tiny pieces to Nimbus.

"Is this seat taken?" A woman with wraparound sunglasses and impressively messy blonde curls slid into the spare seat at the table.

"Um... it is now." Vorana glanced at Zandra, checking to see if she knew this stranger.

Zandra shrugged.

I inhaled deeply. "Sorcha? Is that you under that wig?"

She shushed me and pressed a finger to her lips. "I had to see how many of you are traitors. What a disappointment to find you all here. I should disown you. Friends wouldn't do this to each other."

"Eat delicious food?" I tilted my head.

Sorcha jabbed a finger toward the back of the café. "You choose her over me. We've been friends for ages. I'm wounded."

Vorana's cheeks flushed. "We're not betraying you. We're doing this for you."

"How do you work that out?" Sorcha adjusted her wig, making it lopsided as she scratched underneath it.

"You're worried Verity is using magic to bewitch her customers so they abandon you." Zandra kept her voice low as she glanced around. "We're here to check nothing odd is going on."

"And to sample the fish plate," I murmured.

Sorcha sighed and slumped in her seat. "There's nothing strange going on. I've been here all morning. The food is excellent. And the tea is divine. A house-elf spent ten minutes with me, going through my favorite flavors. What he brought back was something I'd never tasted before. It was incredible. It made me want to laugh and cry at the same time. I instantly ordered a second pot."

"Sounds like magic to me," Sage said.

"That's what I thought!" Sorcha looked around the bustling café. "But I can't find the source. It makes no sense the place is so popular all the time. I got here the second it opened, and there was already a queue of people desperate to get in. It's been like it all morning. I must figure out how to get customers back to my café and pry them free from this horrible place."

"Shouldn't you be at your café?" Vorana asked.

"I closed it for the day. It's a waste of time staying open when this is my competition."

"Don't give up so quickly," I said. "Once people have had their fill of scones and tiny little sandwiches cut into adorable triangles, they'll come back to you."

"Randal said he'd go to your café for lunch," Zandra said.

"Then he'll be disappointed. Although I expect him to sneak in here. After all, it's most likely where he really wants to be." Sorcha scratched under her wig again. "This thing is so irritating."

"Take it off," Zandra said. "Enjoy yourself. There's no point in getting so stressed."

"I'm going to be stressed. It's my livelihood on the line." She finally took off the wig and fluffed her natural hair into shape. "Maybe I should branch out. Or try something new. I thought I had everything sorted at my café, but times are changing. Maybe it's time for me to change, too.

Denver said he wanted a vacation. I could take a couple of weeks off, and we could go away together. Plan the next stage of my life."

"A vacation sounds perfect," I said. "Don't do anything rash, though. We love your café. One little blip shouldn't change the direction of your life forever."

We lapsed into silence as the gorgeous platters of food arrived. Sage's meat platter had me drooling, while my fish smelled like heaven. Everyone, apart from Sorcha, stared with wide-eyed delight at the tiny cream cakes, mini sandwiches, and warm, plump scones.

The conversation remained on mute as we tucked in.

Sorcha scowled at us as she tapped her fingers on the table. "I could open a critter grooming parlor. We don't have one of those in Crimson Cove. I love animals."

"Even the ones that set light to your café's tablecloths." I checked how much Sage had eaten. The bowl was already licked clean. "Do you have the appropriate grooming skills?"

"Sorcha could practice on you." Zandra chuckled at my outraged look.

"Oh, my stars and rainbows! It's you! It's really you."

We all turned to see Verity Yummy standing by the table. She was a curvy redhead, wearing a sugar pink dress, a frilled flowery apron tied around her waist.

Her round cheeks colored a ruddy red. "I'm so sorry, but I couldn't help eavesdropping. It is you, isn't it?"

"Who are you talking to?" Zandra asked.

"You! You're Sorcha Creer." Verity bounced up and down, drawing customers' attention. "Let me give you an enormous hug, you stunning creature."

Sorcha froze in her seat as Verity wrapped her in a huge hug, yanking her out of the chair and off her feet.

"She truly is a monster," I whispered to Zandra. "Just as Sorcha described."

Zandra nodded slowly as she took in the scene, her mouth full of scone.

"I knew it was you under that wig." Verity finally released Sorcha and set her back on her feet. "I've been hiding in the kitchen, terrified you'll hate everything I've created. You don't hate it, do you? Please say you don't. My cream covered heart will break with despair if you do."

"It's ... it's my first time visiting." Sorcha edged back into her seat, panic on her face as she looked to us for support with this overly enthusiastic greeting.

"It's truly an honor to have you here. I love your café, and I modeled my business on it," Verity said.

Sorcha blinked in shock, her mouth open, but no words coming out.

Laughter tinkled out of Verity. "I've been working up the courage to visit your café, but you're so intimidating. A smart, funny, beautiful successful businesswoman. How am I supposed to live up to that?"

"Is it the fangs that intimidate you?" I asked. "Don't worry about them. Sorcha rarely bites unless you really annoy her."

Another tinkle of laughter came out of Verity. "And you have such delightful friends. How lovely. Your lunch is on me. No arguments. My role model is here, and I couldn't be more thrilled. I promise, you'll get the best service. Anything you want, just ask. Nothing is too much trouble." She lurched forward and hugged Sorcha again. "I have a feeling we'll be the best of friends."

Sorcha squirmed in Verity's grip.

"Everyone needs friends," I said.

Verity stood back and clapped her hands together. "And you must be involved in my local tea festival. It could make us oodles of cash. I've been working up the courage to beg you to be involved."

"Why would you need to beg?" Vorana asked.

Verity gestured at Sorcha. "Because she's so busy and popular. Why would she ever notice little old me? I've been so worried it'll be a flop if you're not involved. Please, will you help me make sure it's not a withering disaster?"

"Um..." Sorcha stared at us again.

Vorana shrugged. "It sounds like fun."

Verity blinked like a startled fawn, her focus only on Sorcha. "I'll give you free scones for a month if you say yes. I'll even hand whip the cream myself."

I hopped onto Zandra's shoulder and huffed into her ear. "What are we going to do with such a dreadful monster?"

Chapter 3

Tea leaves

"Did you see the way she tried to crush me?" Sorcha's gaze was fixed ahead as she stomped away from *The English Tea Shoppe*. "My bones were protesting under her evil, unnaturally strong grip. Is she an ogre in disguise? Some kind of goblin? Something brutally strong."

"Most people would have called that a friendly hug." I rode on Zandra's shoulder, the taste of the delicious fish platter the house-elves had served me still lingering like a delicious bouquet I never wanted to fade. "I got the impression Verity wanted to be your friend, not destroy you with an overly-enthusiastic embrace."

"When she touched me, I grew cold," Sorcha said. "There's something wrong with her. Free scones for a month! So much niceness can't be genuine."

"The food was genuinely amazing, even if the niceness was faked." Zandra raised a hand to placate Sorcha when she glowered at her. "You've got to admit the tearoom has a great vibe."

"Some friend you are." Sorcha huffed out a breath. "Vorana, you hated everything about the stupid tearoom, didn't you?"

Vorana slid a guilty glance at Sorcha before looking away. "The house-elves are adorable. And I've never tasted a scone quite like it. So buttery and rich."

"Cake traitor," Sorcha grumbled.

"Verity wants you involved in her local tea event," I said. "She wouldn't have invited you to join in if she didn't like you. She even said she modeled her business on your café. That's quite a compliment."

"I don't believe that. And I can't be involved in her event!" Sorcha said. "I've not discovered it yet, but there's dark trickery at work. All the customers were smiling, and I didn't hear a single complaint from anyone. And everyone was ordering more food. I watched one table devour everything on their plates and order the same thing again. That's disturbingly unnatural."

"I could have gone for another round of scones," Zandra said.

"You're not helping to diffuse this situation," I whispered into her ear.

"Verity is the worst kind of monster." Sorcha bared her fangs and hissed. "Under all that ditzy smiling laughter, there's a heart of pure evil. And I'm going to prove it."

"We should take part in her event," Vorana said after a few seconds of awkward silence as Sorcha set the pace, stomping back to her café. "Verity spoke to me about what she has planned just the other day. It sounds great."

Sorcha slung the wig at her. "Even if I wanted to get involved, which I don't, there's no time to prepare. It's less than a month away."

"Everything is already done," Vorana said. "Verity has organized it all. All you'd have to do is show up to reap the rewards. Just make plenty of delicious food, open your café, and you can sit back and enjoy yourself."

"How do you know so much about this dumb event?" Sorcha snapped.

"I... Well, like I said, Verity talked to me about it. She visited the bookstore and was so excited by its potential."

Sorcha stopped walking and wheeled around to face Vorana. "Potential for what? She's got you under her spell, too?"

"It's not a spell." Vorana glanced at us. "It's a community event full of food, tea, and hopefully books. Verity wants to use my bookstore to hold tea leaf readings."

"Oh! We met a woman in Sorcha's café who was looking for Verity," I said. "She had something to do with tea leaf reading."

Vorana nodded. "Verity said she's getting the very best tea leaf reader to come to Crimson Cove for this event. She wants it to be perfect."

"I hope you said no," Sorcha said. "This is a scam. The stupid tea room, the gross scones, and this ridiculous event."

"It sounds legit to me," Vorana said. "Verity is even paying to use the bookstore for the day. And I'm planning to order in tea leaf reading books and accessories, so if anyone is interested in developing those skills, they can buy everything they need after their reading. It could be fun. And as a bonus, we'll make money out of it."

"I don't trust her," Sorcha said. "How could you betray me like this?"

"This isn't betrayal," I said as gently as I could. "Vorana wants to be part of a community event, which is an excellent idea."

"You be quiet. You've been drugged by Verity's fish," Sorcha snarled. "I know something dodgy is going on."

"Does that mean you won't be a part of the event?" Vorana's hopeful expression faded. "We have a planning meeting tonight at the tea shop. Come along and learn more. Don't make your mind up until you have all the information. Verity has a dozen stores and businesses involved. I know she'd love to have you come along. She thinks you're wonderful. She told me so."

"There's no harm in getting more information," Zandra said. "Even if it's just to confirm your suspicion that she's a monster in disguise."

"I do need to figure out what her angle is," Sorcha said. "I'll come to the meeting, but don't expect me to be friendly."

"We'll attend as backup," I said, and Zandra nodded, obviously realizing there'd be more of Verity's delicious food on offer, and that was an opportunity too good to miss. Even if it meant dealing with Sorcha's surly suspicions for the evening.

"If I could have everybody's attention, please." Verity stood at the front of her quaint tea shop, an excited smile on her face as she quietly clapped her hands. "Thank you all so much for attending tonight. I'm so excited to finalize the plans for our community event. Everyone's business will benefit, and I've already started promoting it, so we'll get visitors from outside Crimson Cove, too."

I was comfortably settled on Zandra's lap, gently making biscuits on her belly. The tea shop was crowded, with representation from all the major shops, including the apothecary, the bakery, and the hotels. I was also happy to have Sorcha sitting next to us, although so far, she'd refused to eat any of the food and had barely greeted Verity, despite receiving another bone-crushing hug when she arrived.

"You all know the main plan for the day," Verity said. "We'll have a guided tour of Crimson Cove, which will include several stops to see if we can find any ghosts at the haunted locations. And we'll be having regular breaks that'll include Tia and Binky's wonderful bakery, Sorcha's perfect café, and, of course, my tiny tearoom. This will give visitors time to buy food and drink and relax. After the guided tours, we'll stop at the apothecary, and then we'll finish at Vorana's beautiful bookstore for an afternoon of browsing and tea leaf reading."

There were murmurs of approval from the assembled group.

Verity turned to the side and held out a hand. "On that note, it gives me the greatest pleasure to introduce one of the world's most skilled and experienced tea leaf readers, Nahla Gerbolt."

There was a small round of applause as the silver-haired woman we'd encountered in Sorcha's café appeared. She wore a stunning black dress with a deep V neckline and gold stars on it that sparkled when she moved.

"Thank you, everybody. You're too kind. I should be the one applauding you all for living in such a charming place." Nahla's voice was a warm, sweet murmur.

Standing behind Nahla to her right was an efficient-looking middle-aged woman in an expensive suit, tapping away on her mobile snow globe. Next to her was a nervous-looking gremlin who kept shuffling his feet, his arms full of papers.

Nahla gently waved away the applause. "Too kind. Too kind. I've met nothing but kindness since I arrived in Crimson Cove. I'll be thrilled to host an afternoon of tea leaf reading. Everyone who pays for a reading will receive half an hour with me."

Sorcha raised her hand. "You won't be able to see many people if you give them so long."

"We can cut the sessions to ten minutes." The woman tapping away on her mobile snow globe barely looked up as she spoke. Her eyes were the brightest green I'd ever seen, one side of her face covered in dragon scales.

"Some customers will only need ten minutes. Some need a little more if their readings are complicated. I want to make sure everyone who attends gets the most value." Nahla glanced over her shoulder at the woman. "Forgive me, I haven't introduced my wonderful team. This is my illustrious agent, Amy Firebrand. I wouldn't be anything if it weren't for her skills."

Amy lifted her chin, acknowledging the group, before returning to her messaging.

"Next to Amy is my loyal personal assistant, Griffin Bumble. He's been with me for over twenty years. I'd be lost without him. He keeps me organized and, most importantly, well fed. I sometimes get so caught up in my tea leaf reading that I forget to look after myself." She gestured to an incredibly handsome man who appeared to be half asleep as he lolled in a comfortable armchair. "And of course, I can't leave out my adorable husband, Ivan. He's been with me since the start of my career, and we often travel together. My team makes me the success I am."

Ivan raised a hand in acknowledgment. He was tall, dark, and handsome, with a slight surfer vibe, his long hair resting on his shirt collar.

"Nahla has kindly agreed to showcase her talents this evening." Verity moved up to join her. "We thought we'd make the short walk from the tearoom to the bookstore and practice setting up. It'll give us a taste of how customers will experience the event. And you never know. You may find out what the future holds for you."

"I've never had my tea leaves read," Zandra whispered to me.

"It's an old-school technique," I said. "I've seen it done plenty of times."

"I suppose you've never had your tea leaves read either. I've never seen you drink tea."

I'd drunk plenty of tea in my time, but not since I'd been turned into a cat. "I'll make the sacrifice to see what the tea leaves reveal."

Zandra grinned. "We'll have to try it out. Especially if the tea comes with some of Verity's delicious cookies."

"Vorana, please stand up," Verity said. "I'm honored you're letting us use your bookstore. Don't be shy. I'm sure everyone in Crimson Cove adores your delightful business almost as much as I do."

Vorana stood, turned, and waved. "Hey, everyone. Happy to be here. Don't really know what else to say." She hurried to sit down again, her cheeks red.

Verity talked about the event's practicalities, which was scheduled to take place three weeks from today. It sounded like she had everything organized, and the more Sorcha listened, the less grumpy she appeared. Perhaps she was softening toward the event. And from what I'd seen of Verity, she was the opposite of a monster. She was generous and kind and only seemed to want to do good.

"Before we go to the bookstore, I have to show everyone these adorable toys Nahla sells." Verity lifted a large stuffed toy cupcake with a smiling face on the front.

Nahla laughed as she picked up her own cupcake. "I got them as a novelty gift, but they've become trendy. I thought children would want them, but adults buy them too. The most magical thing about them is they talk. You can get them to say anything." She squeezed the cupcake.

A sparkle of magic drifted around it, leaving behind the scent of strawberry shortbread. "I'm your best friend. I'm sweet, just like you."

Verity grabbed more cupcakes from a large box and tossed them into the crowd for people to try.

Zandra caught one. She flipped it over a few times. "How does this thing work?"

"Most likely a simple magic spell," I said. "Squeeze it. See what it has to say."

Zandra shrugged and squashed the cupcake.

"Eat me. I'm all yours."

Zandra chuckled.

Nahla's agent, Amy, walked over to where Vorana sat. "Before we use your bookstore, I have to do a full sweep."

"A full sweep for what?" Vorana asked. "I keep the place spotless, if that's what you're worried about."

"Nahla is a top-tier tea leaf reader. Best in the business. She has a rare gift, and it can't be exploited."

Vorana looked startled. "How would I exploit her gifts?"

"I'm not worried about you. I've already run a background check, and it came out clean," Amy said. "But there are unscrupulous people out there. Nahla's readings are always done in private. She can't afford to risk having unauthorized videos of her talent displayed anywhere. Or any recordings. What she gives each client is gifted in confidence."

"It's tea leaves, not world secrets," Zandra said.

Amy sniffed. "It's still important. Nahla's reputation is at stake. The bookstore will have to be checked for recording devices. No unauthorized magic use in there, either."

"I'm happy to help in any way I can," Vorana said. "There are private spaces in the bookstore that would be perfect for Nahla's readings. I've designated them as quiet corners for people to sit and read."

"That should work. I'll look around when we're there this evening." Amy nodded at us and strode away, her gaze already on her mobile snow globe.

"She's scarily efficient," Zandra grumbled.

Vorana shrugged. "I don't mind. She's only doing her job. Protecting her client."

A teapot whirled through the air, slamming against the wall a few inches shy of Nahla's head. She squeaked and ducked as shards of china rained down around her. A second later, the tea shop door was flung open, and a furious woman with jet-black hair and equally black eyes stood in the doorway, magic sparking around her as more teapots lifted and hovered in the air.

She jabbed a finger at Nahla. "Don't believe a word that liar has to say."

Chapter 4

Brewed shock

"Put down those teapots." Amy stood in front of Nahla, her hands raised. Griffin immediately joined her, although he was shaking. He also raised a hand to ward off more teapot attacks.

"Get out of my way unless you want to be hurt," the woman snarled. "I'm not here for you."

"You shouldn't be here at all," Amy said. "There's a restraining order against you."

I glanced at Nahla, who stood stock still, her eyes wide. It was clear these women had met before, and it hadn't been a friendly altercation.

"I care nothing about some stupid restraining order," the teapot-throwing woman said. "I won't stand by and let her deceive anybody else."

"It's fine." Nahla gently pushed Amy aside and moved closer to the woman. "I contacted Petra and told her about the event. I invited her to join us."

"Why do that?" Amy sounded incredulous. "She only ever causes trouble for you."

"Because I want us to get along." Nahla's attention remained on the furious woman. "We're in the same

35

business, so why can't we share? There's plenty of work to go around. And I need an extra pair of hands. Tea leaf reading is exhausting."

"It's a fellow tea leaf connoisseur," I whispered to Zandra.

"And one who clearly hates Nahla," she whispered back.

"There's plenty of room for you at this event," Nahla said to Petra. "All you need to do is turn up on the day and gift the community your incredible talents. The town would love to have you here. So would I."

"You'll do what you always do if I show up. Everyone can see what you're really like." Teapots still swirled around Petra as she kept them afloat with magic.

"I won't tell you again. Calm yourself," Amy said. "We've done this dance before, so you know the outcome. Do you want to spend the night behind bars? You'll only get so many strikes against your name before you're locked up and your career is ruined."

"I don't care if I get arrested," Petra said. "That one is dangerous. The leaves have predicted it."

Nahla's normally bright face contracted. One hand settled over her heart. "What have you seen?"

"I asked the tea leaves to tell me your future," Petra said. "They predicted your downfall. Public ruination. You'll become a mockery to everyone in this community. This will end you. Give up. Stop pretending you do this because you love it. All you care about is the money, merchandising, and sponsorship deals."

Nahla sighed. "I love this work. The tea leaves mean everything to me. And you know, you can't make an accurate prediction about someone else when you make the tea and drink it. Your future was contaminated with mine."

"Which suggests Petra saw her own downfall in those tea leaves," I murmured.

"I'm not sure how accurate tea leaf reading is," Sorcha whispered. "All those strange shapes they allegedly see. Most of the time, they're making it up."

"It's the magic they imbue into the tea that makes it work," I said. "I was once in a teahouse in Peru and saw a woman predict someone's pregnancy. She told her to come back in a week and have another cup of tea, and she'd be able to tell by then if it was a boy or a girl."

"When were you ever in Peru?" Zandra asked.

"It was a while ago. Before we knew each other." I brushed away the fact it was many hundreds of years ago when my form was completely different.

"Please, Petra, let's be friends. I'll set you up a booth in the bookstore, and we can help twice as many people learn their futures," Nahla implored. "It could be fun. Join the event next month, and I'll even make you the headline. That's okay with you, isn't it, Verity?"

Verity nodded slowly, her wary gaze on the spinning teapots.

"We need to discuss this," Amy said sharply. "People are coming to this event because of Nahla. We can't make any last-minute changes. It'll only confuse things. Nahla is the star of the show."

"Petra is as famous as I am in our circles," Nahla said. "Everyone attending will be doubly thrilled to know they have access to two experienced tea leaf readers."

"Everyone will be thrilled," Petra mimicked with a smirk. "I'm so done with your sugary sweetness. It's as fake as those eyelashes."

"I got these eyelashes from my mother. They're all natural." The smile finally slipped from Nahla's face, and her frustration glimmered through.

Amy swatted aside teapots with a swift spell and strode to Petra. She grabbed her elbow and dragged her out of the tea room. "I'll deal with this. You get on with the planning." The door slammed behind them.

Nahla hurried to the window and peered out. "I wish Petra would accept my olive branch. She has so much passion inside her, but it's been warped into an intensely odd hatred for anything I do. I can't understand why she doesn't like me. What have I done to her that was so wrong?"

Griffin joined Nahla by the window, and they watched Amy and Petra arguing outside.

"The world of tea leaf reading is competitive," Vorana said. "I never realized people could get so heated over tea."

"I still don't see the big deal," Sorcha said. "Although I'm interested to know why Petra hates Nahla. And looking at that argument going on outside, Amy knows all the secrets."

Ivan, Nahla's husband, rolled out of the chair he'd been snoozing in and ambled over, his hands tucked into his pants pockets. "Ladies, did I hear something about a bookstore? I've been meaning to pick up a volume about the erotic arts in the Danube."

"What kind of erotic arts are we talking about?" Vorana stared up at him.

"Illicit drawings made while people slept. Apparently, the artist was an expert lock picker. No one knows their identity or anything about them. They'd creep into people's homes and sketch them. The sketches are believed to be highly detailed and always of nudes. Not a stich of bed clothes in sight."

"Um... It's not something I have on the shelf, but if you know the author's name, I can order it in for you," Vorana said. "It'll be here in a couple of days."

Ivan rubbed his hands together, a lazy smile on his face. "That sounds ideal. Shall we go there now? Nahla will be dying to read your tea leaves. She thrives on it. Tea runs through her veins."

"What about Petra?" I asked. "Does she often show up and cause problems for Nahla?"

He lifted one shoulder. "The delightful Petra Petunia Teaping won't be any trouble, not now Amy is sorting things. She's efficient at fixing problems. So, about that book?"

There was no reason to stick around the tea room, so after we'd gathered everybody together, we headed off, leaving Amy and Petra still debating. Nahla asked Amy if she needed any help, but she waved her away and said she had things under control.

I studied Ivan as we walked the short distance to the bookstore. He was weaving from side to side and chuckling to himself. "Does he look well to you?"

"He looks drunk," Zandra said.

Griffin cleared his throat, suddenly appearing beside us. "Ivan is high on life. He enjoys the finer things and has a thirst for experiencing different states of consciousness."

"Do you mean he drinks to excess and takes illegal substances?" Zandra asked.

Griffin flashed a nervous smile. "You didn't hear that from me. Ivan gets bored being on the road. Nahla is always so busy. Her passion is her career, and it comes first. As you may have noticed, Ivan is easy-going, but he needs something to occupy himself when his wife is busy scrying the future."

"So he looks at erotic nudes and gets high," I said. "It's one way to spend your time."

"Don't get me wrong, he's a nice guy. But the only thing he's good for is looking delicious on Nahla's arm. If you'll excuse me." Griffin dashed off and joined Nahla, who was leading the way to the bookstore, with Vorana walking beside her, pointing out the town's interesting features.

Once we were inside the bookstore, Nahla and Vorana headed into the small kitchen at the back to brew heady spiced tea, which we'd drink before getting our tea leaves read. Ivan ambled off, most likely to look for a naughty book to read, while the rest of us settled into comfortable chairs and munched on leftover cookies we'd brought with us from the tea shop. Even Sorcha had a nibble of one and declared it wasn't revolting.

Nahla returned, a pot of tea in her hands. Vorana was close behind her, carrying a tray of mugs. They were passed around, and everyone received their magically brewed tea.

"Griffin, be a dear and summon my tea cauldron," Nahla said. "I want to find it the perfect spot before the event. It may take some time to get it settled."

"Why do you need a cauldron when you can brew your blends in a teapot?" I asked.

"A teapot works fine with such a small group." Nahla held up the pot, watching Griffin as he scurried away, magic already shimmering between his palms. "But for big events, I brew an enormous batch and then get people to scoop out a cup themselves. They make contact with the magic and the tea, and their futures are infused into the blend. It makes large groups easier to work with."

"Are we talking a full-sized cauldron?" Vorana blew on her mug of tea. "I can move the chairs around so you could have it at the front of the store. And I have a movable display that can be shifted too."

"Yes, full-sized. And that location sounds perfect," Nahla said. "Having the cauldron on display will mean anyone passing the bookstore during the event will see what we're doing and be tempted inside."

"We can put signs up in the window and outside as well," Vorana said, catching Nahla's enthusiasm. "Next to the cauldron, we could set up a stand of specialist tea leaf books. If you've got recommendations, I'm happy to order them in so they arrive in time for the event."

"That would be wonderful," Nahla said.

While we were drinking our tea, Griffin reappeared, rolling a large ancient black cauldron in front of him. Nahla dashed over and assisted him, urging caution, while Vorana moved aside chairs to make sure there was enough room. The cauldron was rolled onto its base, and after a moment of shuffling it around, everyone stood back and admired it. It was scuffed, cracked, and with seams of what looked like gold plugging the largest cracks.

Nahla walked outside and peered at it through the window then nodded. She came back in. "Vorana, you're a genius. It looks beautiful there. Well done for making the suggestion."

Vorana blushed. "It was nothing."

"It is everything. This cauldron is my livelihood. It's been in my family for centuries. I'd be lost without it."

"We should get started on the tea leaf reading." Amy appeared in the doorway. "And don't worry. I've dealt with Petra. She won't be a problem anymore."

"Thank you. You're a star," Nahla said. "Now, who's ready to have their tea leaves read?"

Vorana went first and heard only good things about her store and her relationship with Brodie, leaving a smile on her face. Sorcha declined a reading, as did Sage, despite Nahla practically begging them to take part. That left Zandra and me to have our turn.

Nahla sat opposite Zandra and took her empty mug. She swirled it around and tipped it upside down onto a small plate. Then she righted it, tilted it, and looked inside.

"What do the leaves predict?" Zandra asked after a moment of intense silence.

"I see lots of hearts." Nahla smiled up at her. "There are many happy times ahead of you. Your future is full of romance."

Zandra snorted her disbelief.

"The leaves must be showing Randal," I said.

"A boyfriend?" Nahla asked.

"A friend," Zandra said firmly. "We've been friends for ages. We tried dating, but it didn't work. It can't be him."

"Your future is full of love. And it's the romantic kind. Of course, I see the strong and enduring bond you have with your wonderful familiar. It's indicated by this small star. Do you see?"

We peered into the mug, but I couldn't make out a star.

"Anything else?" Zandra asked. "A promotion at work? A sudden windfall of cash?"

"The most prominent thing is a happy ever after. Take comfort in that." Nahla set down the mug and turned her attention to me. "I imagine tea isn't your favorite brew."

"I don't enjoy it, but I'm fine not knowing my future. If I knew everything that was to come, there'd be no surprises."

"I wouldn't mind a few less surprises in my life," Zandra said.

"Since you have such a strong connection to your witch, if you allow me to touch your paw, I may get a reading about your future," Nahla said.

"Go ahead." I held out a paw and gently rested it on her outstretched hand.

She stared at me unblinking then jerked back. "Oh, my."

"What did you see?" Zandra asked. "Juno's not getting in trouble in the future, is she?"

"I... I saw a past of hedonistic glory."

Zandra smirked. "She got up to a few things before we bonded."

Nahla gulped. "And a future of... sadness."

"That's wrong! I'm never sad when I'm with my witch," I said.

Nahla shook out her hand and flexed her fingers. "Let me try again. Perhaps I've muddled my messaging. It can happen when I do several readings one after the other."

I backed away. "I don't need to know my future."

"Hey, Juno, wait," Zandra called out, but I was already hurrying off to sit with Sage.

"Something up?" Sage cracked open one eye.

"Maybe Sorcha is right, and this tea event is a bad idea," I grumbled. "Nahla saw a future full of sadness for me."

"Most likely because you don't get to eat enough fish. There's never enough fish in the world. It makes me grumpy, too. Just the thought of an empty bowl puts me in a bad mood all day."

"Maybe it was that." I settled down, keeping a close eye on Nahla as she talked to everyone about the event. I wasn't willing to accept the future she'd given me.

Sage yawned. "Shall we get out of here?"

"Good idea."

We said our goodbyes and left the bookstore. The moon was rising, and the air was cool as we ambled along the streets, heading home.

"Why do you think she predicted sadness in your future?" Sage asked.

"It was a mistake."

"Nothing troubling you?"

I glanced at Sage. She wasn't one to gossip, and I valued her opinion. "Nahla may have seen the dilemma I'm considering."

"Those dumb stones?"

"Yes! And they're not dumb." I squinted at the moon. "I didn't tell you, but after we helped the dragons, I was gifted another stone. I have all my lost magic. Well, enough of it to make a big difference to my life. If I activate it, everything will change."

"That's what Nahla saw?" Sage asked. "You make that change, and it goes wrong?"

"What could go wrong? I had such power, and so many people adored me. Shouldn't I want that back? Isn't that my right?"

"Everything you've got is already good. Why risk messing it up? You push and get ambitious, and trouble will find you."

I huffed out a breath as we approached Vorana's porch. "Perhaps you're right. But perhaps Nahla was also wrong."

After we got inside the house, Sage instantly fell asleep on the prickly mat by the back door, and I headed to the basement and Zandra's comfy pillow. I kneaded, turned, tried different resting positions, but as hard as I tried, I couldn't sleep.

Although, when I heard Zandra come back from the bookstore with Vorana, I closed my eyes and pretended to snooze.

I hated keeping this secret from my wonderful witch, but I also didn't know how to tell her that our lives would change beyond recognition if I activated my old magic. I wanted to talk to her about this situation, but I needed to find the right time. Somehow, that right time never arrived. And the longer I waited, the harder it got.

Once Zandra was in bed and snoring, I gave up attempting to sleep and headed outside for a moonlit walk. The fresh air would do me good. I'd get my thoughts in order and figure out a way to present this opportunity to Zandra without her thinking everything would change. Or when it did, it would be for the better.

I wandered back to Vorana's bookstore and stopped to admire the giant cauldron in the window. It took my eyes a few seconds to adjust, but when they did, I discovered there were two feet poking out of it.

Chapter 5

Sticky brew

The feet sticking out of the cauldron weren't moving. There was a faint haze of steam rising, suggesting the cauldron had been filled with hot liquid. It was empty when I'd left the bookstore with Sage, but it was possible the group experimented to get more accurate readings.

A little stab of fear pierced my heart. I shook my head. No, those weren't Vorana's shoes. And if something bad had happened to her, Sage would be here. They had a robust bond, and she'd know if her witch was in trouble. And I'd heard Zandra talking to someone when she got home, so she must have returned with Vorana.

I looked around, but at this time of night, the streets were deserted, so there was no one to call over to help. I was tempted to run back home and wake Vorana, but I should check who'd gotten themselves wedged into the cauldron. Perhaps I could rescue them. Although from the lack of movement, it suggested I was too late.

I headed to the door, pressed my paws against it, and used an unlock spell to gain access to the bookstore. The door swung open, and I was met with a heady, herbal aroma that was pungently overwhelming. I stepped inside and paused. The place was silent, suggesting there was nobody else here. At least, nobody else alive.

I hurried to the side of the cauldron. It was full size, so I couldn't see inside it even when standing on my back legs and reaching a paw as far as possible. Fortunately, there was a chair nearby, and after some nudging with my head, I got it close to the cauldron. I hopped onto it and rested my front paws on the edge, but I was still unable to figure out who was inside. Whatever the liquid was, it was murky, and the smell was so offensively intense that a wave of dizziness hit me.

Now I was so close to the feet, I definitely didn't recognize them. Although it was sad someone had perished inside this cauldron, I was glad it was no one I knew.

I nudged one of the feet with a paw. It didn't move. It was very warm. Kind of spongey.

"Let's find something to get you out," I said. "Perhaps a broom. Or maybe I could knock over the cauldron."

I jumped off the chair and shoved the cauldron with both paws. It didn't budge. I thrust a spell at it, and it barely moved. It was no surprise. Since this cauldron was attached to Nahla, her magic would be all over it. And even though she hadn't gotten my tea leaf reading correct, I could tell she had immense abilities.

"Broom it is," I murmured, eager to release the tension by talking to myself. I should be used to finding bodies, since I frequently stumbled across them when I had Zandra by my side, but it was never a pleasant experience.

Five minutes of searching produced no broom, so I returned to the chair and stared into the gross-smelling liquid. I could lift the body with a spell. It would be heavy and covered in strange cauldron magic, so it wouldn't be easy, but it felt wrong to leave her in there. And although I wasn't certain it was a woman, the shoes were a feminine design, so I made the assumption.

I conjured a spell between my front paws and poured it into the liquid. A few bubbles popped on the surface, but the body didn't lift.

"I refuse to be beaten. You will move." I inched closer and tried again. I got more bubbles and an even more unpleasant smell wafting over me. It was a cross between unwashed corpse feet and putrefied cabbage. This magic didn't enjoy being prodded.

I hopped onto the cauldron's edge, fired up the spell, and stuck a paw into the hot liquid. My magic swirled through the cloudy brown fluid, which I could only assume was some form of magically blended tea. There was a hiss, a pop, and steam billowed up. I inhaled a large lungful. My head spun, my heart pounded, and I lost my balance.

A mortified yowl shot out of me as I went under. I bumped against the body and kicked it away. The tea liquid was disturbingly hot, and as hard as I tried not to breathe it in, it flooded my nostrils. I almost passed out as an earthy, hot dead flesh scent overwhelmed me.

I rolled several times, continuing to bash against my dead bathing companion. I kicked and flailed, resisting the desire to yowl again. It took me several tries before I figured out which way was up and launched myself at the edge of the cauldron, throwing a paw over the side before taking a huge inhalation of breath.

I dragged myself out, my glorious white fur drenched and my head still spinning. I rolled off the edge and landed in an undignified heap on the floor, doing nothing but breathing deeply and waiting for my head to stop hurting.

Whatever was in that cauldron was lethal. I'd felt the powerful magic pinging off me, attempting to find a way in. Why use such a strong brew to make simple predictions about the future?

I shuddered, heaving myself up and shaking out my fur, sending manky brown drops of tea everywhere.

Movement outside the store caught my eye, and I soggily squelched toward the window. It was Binky and Archie trotting past. They looked like they were on a mission. I banged hard on the window, making them jump. When they saw me, they hurried over.

Archie poked his huge, furry, hellhound head through the open door. "Juno! You look gross. What are you doing?"

"I had an accident. I could do with some help."

Binky joined him, her furry nose wrinkling. "You stink! What's that gross brown stuff all over your fur?"

"Most likely dead body," I said. "Maybe some tea leaves, too."

"Dead body?" Archie cocked his head, his ears lifting. "You killed someone?"

"No! Come inside. I need to show you something."

Binky shook her head. "We're hunting pixies. We've picked up the scent of a huge group of those irritating little monsters."

"Why hunt pixies? They're irascible creatures but usually harmless."

"For fun," Archie said.

I wrinkled my booping snooter. "You hunt for fun?"

"Sure. Why not?"

"Isn't Remus feeding you enough these days?"

Archie growled fiercely, his teeth exposed. Odd. He was normally the friendliest of hellhounds. "My vampire is perfect. Don't say anything bad about him ever again, or we won't be friends."

"Maybe Juno doesn't need us as friends now she's got a dead body to play with." Binky snickered. "I'm not sure I want to be her friend anyway, since she stinks so bad."

"You'd smell just as unpleasant if you'd landed in a vat of boiling body bits." I narrowed my eyes as they approached. They were filthy and covered in dust. They must have been out hunting for hours to get in such a state.

"You've got us for two minutes," Archie said. "Then we're back after the pixies."

I gestured at the cauldron. "I've been trying to get this body out to find out who it is. I don't think it's anyone local, but—"

Archie barged past me, literally knocking me off my feet. He grabbed one of the legs sticking out of the cauldron and pulled. Binky ran at full speed and slammed into the cauldron, sending it toppling. The contents flooded out across the bookstore, covering Vorana's beautiful rugs with disgusting magical tea blend and boiled fleshy bits.

Archie kept hold of the leg and shook what was left of the body.

"Stop!" I clambered to my paws and dashed over.

He let go of the leg and growled at me. "It's not as if it's harming her. She's long dead."

The body lay face down, so I couldn't see who it was, but I recognized the hair. "Turn her over. Do it gently."

"Who made you the boss?" Binky asked.

"Do it! And I'm not bossing anybody around. Friends help each other."

"Your new friend won't be much help to you." Binky had shoved herself into one of the armchairs to avoid getting her fur wet from the liquid that drenched the floor.

I glared at her, not happy with how much sass she'd suddenly developed. Binky was usually a sweetheart.

Archie grumbled to himself then flipped the body over with one large paw.

I let out a slow breath. "As I thought. Nahla Gerbolt."

"I don't know her." Archie was already heading to the door.

"She came to Crimson Cove because she was involved in Verity's tea event," I said, still looking at the body. "Nahla read tea leaves."

"If she was any good, she'd have predicted this and not be dead." Binky joined Archie by the door. "Juno, you need a bath. Your fur is turning brown."

I glanced at my fur to discover there were sticky brown clumps of goo all over me. I went to lick it off then stopped. Although it was likely herbs from the tea brew, there could be bits of dead tea leaf scryer attached to me. I'd need Zandra's help to have a thorough bath as soon as possible.

"Could one of you—" I shrieked as an intense pain reared up my spine, digging into my skin.

"What's up with you?" Archie stared at me as I fell on my side and writhed.

I couldn't speak, only howl as the pain grew worse, splinters of agony stabbing into my behind.

"Wow! Juno, your tail's growing back." Binky trotted over and sniffed me.

"Make it stop," I forced out. "Too painful."

"Look. It's almost done growing." Binky unhelpfully batted at my butt with a paw, sending another wave of pain up my spine and into my head.

I must have blacked out for a few seconds because, when I came to, I was on my side, far too close to Nahla's bright pink body for comfort. Archie and Binky were play-fighting by the door, not seeming bothered by my struggles.

But the pain was gone. I weakly lifted my head and wheezed a startled laugh. My tail was back! My glorious, fluffy pride and joy had returned. Why? I glanced at the cauldron. Could it be whatever was in there had prompted my tail's return?

As tempting as it was to lie on my side and feel sorry for myself, the floor was damp and sticky with brewed tea, and a corpse lay next to me, so I clambered to my feet, staggering slightly.

"Hey! She's not dead." Binky looked over at me. "We were only hanging around to see if you made it. Archie wanted to know what you'd taste like."

I shook my head, still dizzy from the magic and the shock. "I don't understand."

"He wanted to eat you," Binky said. "I said he should wait to see if you made it. We didn't want you fighting back. All that weird power you have freaks me out."

"I'm glad it does." I hissed. "Archie, don't ever think about eating me again."

He growled. "I'm bored. Let's get out of here. We need to hunt down more pixies."

"Wait! You need to tell the angels what we found. This may not have been an accident," I said.

"Angel Force. What a joke," Binky said. "Those morons can't find their way out of a paper bag when they're given directions and head torches."

"Nahla may have been pushed into the cauldron," I said. "This could be a murder scene."

"If it is, we've messed it up," Binky said. "You most of all. You went swimming in the cauldron before we even arrived."

I winced. I hadn't been thinking clearly. I blamed the pungent tea aroma. If I hadn't inhaled that lungful, I wouldn't have slipped in and gotten confused. It may have given me back my tail, but I wasn't sure it was worth it. "Please. I need your help. I'll stay with the body."

Binky shrugged. "If we pass Angel Force, we'll knock and run."

"Let's go. I smell pixie." Archie bounded out of the door, and Binky raced after him. Fortunately, if they stayed on that path, they'd run past the Angel Force office. I had to hope they kept their word and alerted the angels to the dead body problem.

Although I couldn't rely on them, since they were behaving so oddly. They were usually friendly, but they'd been mean and hadn't wanted to help. And I couldn't believe Archie only stuck around to see if I died so he could eat me. What was wrong with my friends?

I looked at my tail and twitched it. "Hello, old friend. At least one decent thing has come out of this tragedy." It would be good to be able to balance properly. If I'd had my tail when I'd looked into the cauldron, I wouldn't have fallen in.

I hopped onto the chair next to the cauldron because the floor was unpleasantly sticky and stinky. I was desperate for a wash, but the last thing I wanted to do was ingest any of this strange potent tea blend. I settled on the chair, a light orb hovering over me, and looked around. There were no signs of a struggle, so perhaps this had been an accident. The door into the bookstore was locked when I arrived, so no one had broken in. But that left the question of what was Nahla doing here on her own. And did she slip, or was she pushed?

There were two thuds outside the bookstore. Cythera and Bertoli had landed. They shook out their wings and hurried over.

Cythera strode through the doorway. She looked around before shaking her head, her annoyed gaze settling on me. "Juno! Whose death are you involved in this time?"

Chapter 6

Stinky tail

"It is strange how often I find myself in these deadly predicaments," I said. "Some would say it's lucky. Lucky for you. If I weren't here, you'd never figure out what was going on."

Cythera's wings fluttered her displeasure, her sharp gaze on the flooded floor. "Is it safe to come in?"

"Provided you don't mind getting sticky tea blend all over those white boots," I said. "As you can see, it stains." I did a turn for her so she could see my ruined fur.

"You got your tail back!" Bertoli was peering around Cythera, taking in the scene.

"As if by magic. Let me catch you up on a few things." I inhaled, preparing myself to weave the extraordinary story of how I discovered Nahla dead in a scolding cauldron of magical tea.

"I'm only interested in the body." Cythera tiptoed her way across the sticky floor. "Who is it?"

"Nahla Gerbolt. She was here for Verity's community tea event. Apparently, Nahla was an expert tea leaf reader."

Cythera looked around. "She got into a fight with someone? They've made a mess of Vorana's bookstore."

"Ah! Some of this mess is down to me. And Archie and Binky. They were kind enough to tip over the cauldron so we could get Nahla out. I wanted to make sure there was no hope of resuscitation before giving up on her."

Cythera swirled a finger in the air. "You made this mess?"

"I tried to extract Nahla from the cauldron, but I couldn't find a suitable object to pry her out, and my magic surprisingly had little effect. I whacked the liquid with a powerful spell, and that's when I toppled in. I almost drowned."

"There must have been powerful magic in that cauldron." Bertoli was tiptoeing around the scene, too. "To knock you out and then give you a new tail."

"And let's not forget, kill a woman," Cythera said.

"Oh! Of course." Bertoli looked at me. "Do you know how powerful Nahla was?"

"Apparently, she was one of the best tea leaf readers in the business," I said. "Although I experienced her talents and was less than impressed. She gave an inaccurate reading of my future. And she said Zandra would have a life full of romance."

Cythera smirked. "It sounds like she had no clue how to read tea leaves. Where is Zandra, anyway?"

"I left her at home. I couldn't sleep, so I took a walk."

"And your walk brought you here?"

"We'd spent the evening at the bookstore. Vorana is involved in the community tea and cake event Verity is planning. We got together to talk tactics and have our tea leaves read. I left early with Sage, and the others stayed."

"What did they do?" Cythera peered at Nahla's body.

"I didn't ask Zandra when she came back."

"Why not? Are you fighting?" Cythera asked.

"No fight. I wasn't in the mood for conversation. She went to sleep, and I went walking. And you must be glad I did. If Nahla had been left to brew all night, there'd be nothing left for you to examine."

Cythera grimaced. "Where are Binky and Archie?"

"Gone. They passed by the bookstore, and I called them in to help," I said. "Did you notice anything strange about them when they stopped at Angel Force to give you the news?"

"Archie has always been odd," Cythera said. "And Binky has a troubled past. She almost had to be put down because she was considered dangerously unstable."

"They're perfectly adorable. Well, they used to be. But Archie was prickly, and Binky was behaving out of character. They said they were hunting pixies."

"They'd better not be." Cythera settled her hands on her hips and scowled. "With all this mess, there's little we can learn about what happened. I don't see any obvious injuries on the body, so it could have been an accident."

"I wondered that, but Nahla had years of experience, and you can tell her cauldron is ancient. What would make her suddenly slip when she's so used to working with it?"

"Juno! Is that you in there?" Zandra stood in the open bookstore doorway, still dressed in her pajamas, her hair messy. Behind her were Vorana and Sage.

"Greetings. What are you all doing here?" I asked.

"I had a nightmare," Zandra said. "I thought you were drowning. And you do look half drowned. What's that muck on your fur?"

"That's what we were figuring out," Cythera said. "Not the muck. This. You can't come in. We have a potential crime scene."

"What happened to my store?" Vorana asked in wide-eyed horror. "Has there been a flood?"

"I'll fill you in while we let the angels work." I skipped across the sticky floor and leapt onto Zandra's shoulder.

She grimaced and jerked her head away before plucking a chunk of brown sticky goo off my fur. "What the heck is this? Mud? It smells gross."

"I fell into the cauldron. Let me explain." I took a few minutes to fill everyone in on the unfortunate goings-on in the bookstore. The whole time I talked, Zandra held her nose and refused to let me lean against her face.

"I don't understand." Vorana's face was pale by the time I'd finished. "We all left the bookstore at the same time. After you and Sage went home early,

Nahla fired up her cauldron. We filled it, and she put in herbs and spells and mixed it. It brewed for half an hour, and then we had our tea leaves read again."

Bertoli had been listening to the conversation while Cythera examined the scene. "Nahla didn't stay behind while the rest of you went home?"

Vorana shook her head. "No, it was getting late by the time we were done. She left the cauldron in the window full of brewed tea. She said it would be fine overnight, and she'd use the liquid tomorrow to do more readings. Apparently, the longer you leave it, the stronger it gets."

"It was certainly pungent when I inhaled it," I said.

"I can't figure out how Nahla got back in," Vorana said. "I was the last to leave, and I know I locked the door."

"She must have used magic to get inside," I said.

"Where was Nahla staying?" Bertoli asked.

"She didn't say, but there's not much choice in Crimson Cove." Zandra sounded nasally since she was still pinching her nose shut. "I can't imagine she travels cheap, so probably the Sleepy Stardust Sanctuary would be a good place to start."

"She was traveling alone?" Cythera joined us by the door.

"No, she had her agent, Amy, and an assistant, Griffin, with her," I said. "They were here this evening."

"Did you notice any problems between them?" Cythera asked.

"Nothing like that," I said. "Everyone was focused on the upcoming event. It was all pleasant conversation and tea. Why do you ask? Have you found something to make you think this wasn't an accident?"

"I'm covering all the bases," Cythera said. "We already know about the planned tea festival, though, and everything seemed aboveboard when the license came through. The name Amy sounds familiar, too. I believe she sent in paperwork. She requested an Angel Force presence because she was worried about crowd control. Nahla was a big deal in her specialism, and Amy didn't want her getting mobbed while she was here."

"Did you think there was anything odd about that request?" I asked.

"It seemed fine," Cythera said. "And I had no problem with loaning two angels as a show of support."

Vorana had been quiet, taking in the devastation in her store. "I'm not sure I'll be able to take part in the event. It'll take weeks to clear this up."

"You definitely won't be opening tomorrow," Cythera said. "We need to process everything in case something unfortunate happened here."

"I wouldn't open anyway with the floor so wet. And that strange smell won't encourage customers," Vorana said. "I doubt I'll get any at all when they learn some poor tea leaf reader drowned in her own cauldron."

"I'm always surprised by people's morbid curiosity," I said. "Death attracts interest. Don't be surprised if you get a rush of customers coming in to see the scene."

"People can be so distasteful," Cythera said. "But the fluffy is right."

"Oh! Your tail is back." Zandra lifted me and held me in front of her. "I knew there was something different about you. I got so caught up in the weird stink that I missed it."

"It grew back after I fell into the cauldron," I said. "Whatever magic is in there regenerated my tail. Isn't it pretty?"

"That fall also turned you into a super stinker," Sage said. "Why did you have to fall in? You'll make the whole house smell rancid for days."

"I already told you, my magic activated an unpleasant spell. There was something nasty in that cauldron that didn't want to be disturbed. I disturbed it, and it fought back."

Zandra picked another lump of brown goo out of my fur. "I don't know how we'll get this all off."

"A powerful cleansing spell may do the trick," Vorana said.

"Stop worrying about the fluffy's fur," Cythera said. "We need to get to the bottom of what happened here. Vorana, you're certain you locked all the doors before leaving?"

"Absolutely. I always check."

"Maybe you left a window open or a door unlocked at the back."

"No, I have a routine I follow at the end of every day."

"She does," Sage said. "I follow her around to make sure it's done properly."

"You weren't here last night," Cythera said. "You left early with Juno. Perhaps Vorana missed something."

Vorana chewed on her bottom lip. "I don't think I did. But now you say that, I'm having doubts."

"I watched you turn the key in the door," Zandra said, "and check the handle. It was locked."

"If that's true, then it means Nahla snuck back here for a reason," Cythera said. "Could it have been to meet somebody?"

"She didn't say anything to me," Vorana said. "But if she planned on sneaking inside without my permission, she'd have kept it to herself."

"She made no mention to me about catching up with anyone," Zandra said. "And we stayed until past eleven, so everyone was ready for bed."

"Nahla found tea leaf readings tiring, so it's unlikely she came back here to do more of them," Vorana said.

"An affair?" Bertoli suggested. "She was meeting a lover and didn't want anyone to know."

"Nahla seemed happily married," I said. "Her husband, Ivan, is also here. And I don't think she'd been to Crimson Cove before because Nahla didn't know where the teashop was when she stopped by Sorcha's café, so she wouldn't have had a secret boyfriend stashed here."

Cythera turned to Bertoli. "Find out where Nahla's party is staying. We need to question them all to discount foul play. But looking at this scene, as much as we can, thanks to Juno's interference, I believe this to be an accident. Nahla was tired, she got overwhelmed by that stench coming out of the cauldron, and she tripped. She fell in and couldn't get out. She may even have been unconscious by the time she went under."

"Don't be so quick to rule it an accident," I said. "We still haven't figured out why she came back here."

Cythera sighed. "I'm not. Did any of you have a problem with Nahla?"

"We didn't know her," Zandra said. "She seemed nice enough in the time we spent with her."

"Oh! What about Petra?" Vorana asked. "If we're looking for a troublemaker, she'd fit the mold."

"Who's Petra?" Cythera asked.

"Petra Teaping. Another tea leaf reader," I said. "She arrived when we were at Verity's teashop earlier this evening, stormed in, and attacked Nahla. She threw a teapot at her."

"They were business rivals?"

"They must have been. Petra hated Nahla. And Amy said there was a restraining order, so Petra shouldn't have been in the same room as her."

"We can check that. See what the restraining order relates to," Cythera said.

I nodded along as they discussed Petra and where they might find her. Even though Cythera was swaying toward Nahla's death being an accident, I was yet to be convinced. Maybe Petra decided she wanted to steep her competition for good.

Chapter 7

Irksome angel

I rolled over and did a full-body stretch, pausing for a moment to admire my gloriously fluffy tail. How I'd missed it. I felt complete again with my tail. Even though the magic in Nahla's cauldron had been deeply unpleasant to bathe in, I was thrilled with this result.

I stretched again and sniffed my fur. Despite the two sink baths provided by Zandra after we got home last night, I smelt strange. Slightly moldy. Nahla's magic must have been super strong to linger for so long. And when I looked closely, there were still faint brown splodges on my white fur. I needed to figure out how to get that removed, but right now, I had bigger things to worry about.

I shuffled off the pillow, turned in a circle, and rested my behind on Zandra's face. That was a sure way to wake her in the morning.

"Get your butt off my face," she mumbled. "It's grossly unhygienic."

"I'm squeaky clean after last night's bathing fun. Look at my tail. It's so beautiful." I draped it over her forehead.

"Off!"

I turned around, deciding instead to make biscuits on Zandra's belly.

She grunted when I jumped on her. "What's got you so excited this morning?"

"Nothing in particular. I'm feeling positive about today. And I've been thinking about Nahla."

"Finding a dead body stuffed in a cauldron of hot liquid makes you happy?" Zandra rested a hand on my head, her eyes still closed.

"No, that was a tragedy. But I think the return of my tail is a sign of good things to come."

She grunted. "If you say so."

"Don't go back to sleep." I jumped up and down on Zandra's stomach to make sure she didn't snooze. "We should visit Angel Force before we start work to see what's going on with Nahla."

"Why bother? I agree with Cythera. Nahla was just clumsy and made a mistake. That mistake got her killed."

"We don't know that for certain," I said. "She wasn't drinking when we were at the teashop or the bookstore. Other than tea, and we all had that. And she didn't seem unwell. Why would she suddenly lose her balance and plunge to her death in her own concoction? What if there's more to this mystery?"

"If there is, let the angels deal with it," Zandra said. "We have work. The animals are still being weird. We've had to deal with twice the number of jobs every day. And that's even making Barney and Ember grumpy. And Ember is always irritatingly cheerful."

"Could the unstable behavior shifting through the animal population be contagious?" I asked. "Last night, at the bookstore, Archie and Binky weren't themselves. Binky believed Archie wanted to eat me!"

"Perhaps his feral hellhound side is coming out," Zandra said. "We can't forget what he really is. And he spends all of his time with Remus. He's hardly a great influence."

"Remus wouldn't encourage Archie to eat anyone who didn't deserve it," I said. "Besides, Remus is mainly benevolent with a side order of sassy vampire."

"Perhaps Archie sees you as more of a tasty treat than a friend these days," Zandra said. "I know you think you're indestructible, but you're only a small cat."

I softly growled and stabbed my claws into her belly, making her jump. "You know not to underestimate me. So does Archie. We should insist he get tests done to see if we can figure out why he's behaving oddly. Depending on the results, Archie could help us get to the bottom of the unrest in the town's animal population."

"Who's going to authorize that? Or pay for it?" Zandra yawned noisily. "We're overworked, underpaid, and never appreciated. I've been thinking we need a career change."

I paused. "Leave animal control?"

"Have a complete fresh start," Zandra said.

"A fresh start suggests a move. You don't want to move away from Crimson Cove, do you?"

"Why not?"

"We have a life here. Friends. Family. I have Sammy. And your mother is getting married. You need to be around for that."

"She was never much of a mother to me," Zandra said. "Why should I put myself out to help her?"

I turned around, so I faced Zandra. "Your relationship has been less than perfect, but she did her best when raising you."

"Whatever you say. But you weren't around. You don't know what it was like."

"In a way, I do. My bond gives me access to most of your emotions."

"Keep your paws out of my emotions," Zandra said.

I jerked back in surprise at her sharp tone. "You need to give this serious thought. We're settled. Happy. And you'd miss Randal, wouldn't you?"

Zandra lifted me off her belly and set me on the bed before rolling out from under the covers and onto her feet. "Don't believe the dead tea leaf woman's predictions. If anything was going to happen between me and Randal, it would have done so by now. We're not interested in each other like that."

Concern flickered through me as Zandra went into the bathroom to shower and dress. She'd never talked about leaving Crimson Cove. Before we'd settled here, she'd been a prickly, erratic witch, even with my calming influence. It wasn't until we'd put down roots and integrated into this community that she seemed happier. To uproot and start again would be stressful. Where did this desire come from?

After Zandra was dressed, we headed up the basement stairs and into the kitchen. Vorana and Sage were already in there. Vorana was flipping pancakes, and Sage was in her usual seat, eagerly awaiting breakfast.

Vorana pointed at a teapot on the table. "I thought we'd have some of Nahla's blended tea with our breakfast. She was an ambassador to three different tea companies and gave each blend a hint of magic. It'll be a nice way to commemorate her."

"Sounds good to me." Zandra settled into a seat. "So long as it comes with a stack of those pancakes."

"Of course. They're almost ready."

I nodded a greeting at Sage as I clambered into my chair. I was happy to see there were pieces of bacon already fried and waiting for us on the counter.

Once everyone had their breakfast in front of them, Vorana settled in her seat, poured tea, and lifted her cup. "Here's to Nahla Gerbolt. We didn't know her for long, but I'm sorry about what happened to her. Let's hope she's at peace."

Vorana and Zandra drank their tea. I sniffed the saucer of tea in front of me. It smelled earthy with a honey under-tang. I wasn't in the mood for tea, so I politely ignored it, as did Sage, who was chomping on a large slice of bacon.

"This is delicious," Zandra said after she'd drained her cup. "Almost as good as cake."

"I thought the same!" Vorana said. "I can't get enough of the stuff. I don't know what kind of magic

Nahla used in her tea blends, but this is incredible. If you want, I can make you a flask you can take to work."

"That's a plan I approve of." Zandra shoved half a pancake into her mouth and chewed.

"I was just saying we should go to Angel Force and see how the investigation into Nahla's death is progressing," I said to Vorana.

Zandra shook her head. "We're not chasing another case. We're way too busy at work. You know that. Stop trying to get Vorana on side and guilt me into helping."

"It's a shame you can't skip work for the day," Vorana said. "I won't be able to open the bookstore until the dead body energy has been cleansed from the place. And it'll take a while for the floors to dry. I could also do with some help to check the stock and see what was damaged. Then I need to contact the insurance and get them involved. I'm hoping they don't take too long to fix things."

"I'm not into dealing with dead body energy," Zandra said.

"We've encountered plenty of dead body energy," I murmured.

Zandra ignored me. "Can't you mask the mess under a spell until the repairs take place?"

"I'll try, but I'm not sure I can rid the store of that funky smell. Maybe closing for a few days will be enough to right things. I need to make sure my customers don't stick to the floor when browsing."

"It is curious what happened at your bookstore. Why did Nahla go back there?" I asked.

Vorana shook her head. "Beats me. I wish she'd stayed away, though."

As much as I wanted to persuade Zandra that we should look into this mysterious death, from the stubborn set of her jaw and her refusal to discuss the subject, she wasn't for turning. Perhaps she'd feel differently once we'd done a morning of work. If things weren't busy, we'd easily have time to drop in to see Cythera and Bertoli and get an update. When Zandra learned more about the case, she may become interested.

Five minutes later, we were heading to the front door, and Zandra was yelling goodbyes to Vorana and Sage. She pulled open the door. Cythera stood outside, her expression set to grim.

"Greetings!" I said. "I was just thinking about you, and here you are. It's as if I magicked you onto Vorana's front porch."

Cythera's expression remained stony. "Why did you all conceal a fight Sorcha had with Verity?"

I froze, one front paw in the air. Why was she asking that question?

"What makes you think they fought?" Zandra's tone was cautious, sensing Cythera was sniffing for trouble to lie at Sorcha's feet.

Cythera marched into the house without an invitation, and we followed her along the hallway and into the kitchen.

"Hey, Cythera," Vorana said. "There are pancakes going spare if you'd like some."

"I'm not here for the free food." Her gaze flicked to the pancakes. "Last night at the bookstore, none of you told me about Sorcha having issues with Verity."

Vorana glanced at Zandra. "What would have been the point of that?"

"They fight, and Nahla ends up dead that same evening. I'm not a fan of coincidences," Cythera said. "Tell me what happened between Sorcha and Verity."

I jumped onto the kitchen table. "The way you're talking, it suggests you have concerns about Sorcha, although I can't imagine why. She's always been good to Angel Force."

Cythera paced the kitchen, her giant wings aflutter. "Here's my thinking. Sorcha hates Verity. Verity is arranging a special event for the town. She invites Nahla to get involved, and Sorcha sees a chance to ruin the event by killing Nahla."

"That's a giant leap you've made." I stared up at Cythera in shock. She often came to the wrong conclusions but was rarely one to pull radical theories out of the air.

"Customers from Sorcha's café claimed she was complaining about Verity. She despised her."

"What customers?" I asked. "They've abandoned Sorcha for the new teashop."

"Ah-ha! That information only confirms my suspicions about Sorcha's motive. She hates Verity for destroying her business, so she kills Nahla to ruin Verity's event and plans to frame her for said murder."

I resisted the urge to roll my eyes. "A few bad weeks at the café won't have convinced Sorcha to murder Nahla. They barely knew each other."

"And if Sorcha hated Verity, she'd kill her," Vorana said. "Not that Sorcha has killed anybody. Besides, Verity and Sorcha were becoming friendly."

"I didn't notice that last night," Zandra said.

Vorana gathered empty plates and mugs from the table. "Sorcha is even considering getting involved in the tea festival."

"You're telling me I've been lied to?" Cythera snapped.

Vorana nodded cautiously. "Sorcha was unhappy with Verity for taking customers from her, but she knew the interest would wear off. And she had no problem with Nahla."

"Cythera, you know Sorcha. This isn't how she moves." I looked at Zandra to back me up.

She leaned against the kitchen counter and undid the flask Vorana had given her full of tea. She poured herself a cup and took a sip. "Sorcha didn't want Nahla to read her tea leaves. She refused a reading."

"What does that have to do with these wild accusations Cythera has come up with?" I couldn't believe Zandra was so quick to point out an issue between Sorcha and Nahla. Did she want her friend to look guilty of murder?

"I'm just saying maybe Sorcha is hiding something. She was worried what the tea leaves would reveal," Zandra said.

"Sorcha doesn't have secrets." Vorana shot a sharp look at Zandra. "We share everything."

"Maybe you're all involved," Cythera said. "After all, this fluffy found the body."

"Involved in what, exactly?" I asked. "Last night, you were leaning toward Nahla slipping into her cauldron and drowning. What changed your mind?"

"I wasn't settled on that theory," Cythera said. "It was the simplest solution, which is sometimes the best thing to focus upon."

"Something prompted this curious line of questioning," I said.

"There's nothing curious about my expertise."

"So..."

Cythera scowled at me. "I spoke to Nahla's agent, Amy, and she said how highly regarded Nahla was. Some people were threatened by her talents."

"And you think Sorcha was threatened by her?" Cythera was making barely any sense. She usually followed a path of logic, even when it was the wrong logic, but this path was full of sharp turns and scary dead ends that led straight to an innocent friend. "Where are you going with this?"

"Having spoken to those closest to Nahla and worked through the information we have so far, I don't believe Nahla's death was an accident," Cythera said. "And since Sorcha had an issue with Verity and wanted to ruin her, why not murder the star of her tea festival? Sorcha was hoping she could frame Verity and get rid of that problem, too."

I batted at Cythera's wing with a paw. "You're being irrational. Are you sure you don't want any food? Perhaps low blood sugar is making your thought patterns wonky."

Cythera swatted me off the table with the same wing, and I landed on the floor. Thankfully, now I had my marvelous tail back, my balance was perfect, so I landed on all four paws and shook out my fur.

"I wouldn't be so suspicious of Sorcha if she hadn't disappeared," Cythera said.

"What do you mean?" Vorana asked. "We saw her last night."

"I went to her home, and she's gone."

"Gone? Did she take her things with her?" I asked.

"No, well, not that I could see," Cythera said. "But she wouldn't open the door. I knocked for ten minutes and demanded to be let in. She refused."

I sighed. "Sorcha isn't missing, and she didn't refuse you anything. She does daily dawn yoga with Denver at Remus's mansion. Apparently, Denver's most flexible just before bed, so they get together for half an hour of stretching before he tucks himself away in his coffin. Although, I actually think he has a most comfortable room with blackout blinds in the windows, so the sun doesn't bother him. Anyway, Sorcha hasn't fled. She's doing the downward facing dog with her sweetie."

Cythera frowned, suggesting she found that information most unhelpful to her unfounded and ridiculous belief Sorcha was a cold-blooded killer who murdered someone to ruin a tea festival. "It's all suspicious. And I don't like it."

"Sorcha can't be a serious suspect in Nahla's death," I said. "Have you questioned Petra? Having witnessed how angry she got with Nahla, if foul play was involved, she must be considered your prime suspect."

"We're interviewing her soon," Cythera said. "She's willingly coming into Angel Force in a few hours."

"We'll be there," I said.

Cythera opened her mouth to protest, but I cut her off.

"Sorcha can't get in trouble because you're not thinking straight." I ducked as a giant white wing swooped down on me and skittered over to Zandra.

This whole time, she'd barely said two words and had simply sipped on her flask of tea, seeming more bored by the conversation than surprised Sorcha was being considered as a murder suspect.

I clambered onto her shoulder to avoid being whacked with Cythera's wing again. "We'll help Sorcha, won't we?"

"Sure. If she needs helping," Zandra said. "What time's the interview?"

"Petra is arriving at noon," Cythera said. "But I don't need your interference."

"Clearly you do, if you're considering Sorcha as a murder suspect," I said. "We'll be there to fix this muddle."

"Perhaps I'll let you in. Perhaps I won't. When Sorcha shows up, send her to me." Cythera turned and marched out of the kitchen, slamming the front door behind her.

Vorana stood, her expression anxious. "We need to warn Sorcha she's on Angel Force's radar for a crime she didn't commit."

I nodded, but Zandra simply shrugged. "You do that. We need to get to work." She collected her flask, and we headed out of the house.

"Aren't you worried about Sorcha?" I asked. "Surely we can spare a few minutes to help her."

"Everything's under control. You worry too much. Focus on our problems, not someone else's."

I was worried. Not only about Sorcha and Cythera's unfounded interest in her but also why my witch was behaving anything but wonderfully.

Chapter 8

An obvious suspect

"We need to go, or we'll be late." I hopped onto the incident report Zandra was filling in after we'd had a near miss with a green speckled primate that narrowly escaped our clutches in a flurry of fur and fury.

"Late for what? Lunch? We can eat when I'm done." She gently nudged me off the form.

"Petra's interview at Angel Force. Cythera said it's happening at noon. I want to hear what she has to say. She's obviously the prime suspect if it turns out Nahla was murdered. And we need to be there to ensure Cythera doesn't remain focused on Sorcha."

"Do we really? Cythera usually comes to her senses."

"Only with nudging from us," I said. "Sorcha's a friend. When did you stop caring about her?"

Zandra checked her empty flask and frowned. "I'm getting old and jaded."

"That's a possibility. The number of times you've been to the bathroom since we got here suggests you're racing toward middle-aged lady bladder problems."

"My bladder is fine! It's all this tea Vorana gave me. It's so tasty that I can't stop drinking it."

"It's all gone now." I hopped onto the form again and batted at her pen. "Finish that report later. We need to get to Angel Force."

Zandra scribbled a few more lines then huffed out her displeasure as we left animal control. "I don't see what the fuss is about. This is something and nothing."

"Let's make sure it remains nothing when it comes to Sorcha," I said. "Or she could find herself behind bars. And that's unacceptable."

I cajoled Zandra every step of the way to get to Angel Force in time. After we'd signed in, we headed through to the open-plan office full of desks for the angels to work at when they weren't out solving crimes and saving the day. Cythera was just leading Petra into an interview room. She glared at us and jabbed a finger at the room next door where we could watch through the one-way glass.

"Waste of time," Zandra muttered as she trudged into the room.

"If you behave, we can go back to Vorana's and get more of that weird tea. But not another word of complaint about helping a friend, or I'll make you drink tepid tap water all afternoon."

That enticement finally stopped the grumbling, and Zandra sank into a chair. Rather than sitting on her lap, I sat in an empty chair. I didn't like being around my witch when she behaved like this.

Cythera was conducting the interview with Bertoli, who had a notepad ready to record details, while Cythera ran through the usual task of getting Petra's full name and address.

"Could you tell us about your particular magic specialty?" Cythera asked.

"I predict people's futures through reading their tea leaves." Petra appeared less angry than the last time I saw her, and her eyes were no longer pools of intense hatred.

"Is that an exact magic?"

"It predicts possible futures based on a number of factors," Petra said. "Although sometimes, the person's mood will affect the reading. If they've had a bad day, it's harder to discover positive futures. It's more of an art than a science, but my prediction rate is one of the highest in the business. I'm excellent at reading people."

"The tea leaf business is nonsense," Zandra whispered. "Nahla saw romance in my future when it's never going to happen."

"It won't happen if you remain so sullen," I murmured.

"I'm not sullen. I just don't want to do this."

"Nahla also read tea leaves, didn't she?" Cythera asked.

"Unfortunately, she did. Our paths crossed many times at events."

"Why do you say unfortunately?"

"Nahla would steal clients. Not just mine."

"She won't be doing that anymore," Cythera said.

Petra looked away for a second. "I'm sorry about what happened to her. We weren't friends, but that can't have been a fun way to go. I've experienced her magic when she reads tea leaves, so I know she doesn't mess around. She created exacting blends to ensure she gave customers the best possible reading. It left her exhausted, but it was strong magic."

"The two of you have a tangled history," Cythera said. "We pulled your file. Three separate restraining orders have been filed against you because of your problems with Nahla."

"I had my reasons for despising her," Petra said. "But our problems go back years, and in that time, I've never once tried to kill her."

"What are your reasons for disliking her so intensely?"

Petra huffed out a breath. "Nahla always had everything handed to her on a plate. She never had to work to be successful. Some of us never got that luxury. She comes from a wealthy family, and they paid for her education, her internship at the Spiced Tea Company so she could hone her craft, and then they set her up in her own business. Since then, she's made a fortune."

"You don't think Nahla deserved that success and fortune?" Cythera asked.

"Like I said, her success is because of the wealth and influence behind her. When you don't have that, it's harder to succeed. The magical tea blends we use are expensive and hard to get hold of. I'm limited to how many readings I can do based on the supplies I have. Lucky old Nahla had an endless supply of tea. Of course, she'd become more successful than any of us."

"Are you suggesting she wasn't well-liked in your community?"

"There are plenty of us who had issues with her. She'd occasionally throw out a token of support, pretend she wanted us involved at the events she lorded over, but she wanted to be the best, and she'd step on anyone who came close to getting in her way."

"Petra is being open about how much she despised Nahla," I said.

"She wouldn't be so honest if she was guilty," Zandra said. "Let's stick with the accident theory and get out of here."

"We'll listen for a few more minutes," I said. "At least Cythera is asking sensible questions. She must have had a change of heart about Sorcha's guilt."

"Or you browbeat her enough that she feels obliged to ask these dumb questions."

I slid some serious side eye at my witch but didn't comment.

"When did your problems with Nahla begin?" Cythera asked.

"She first got in my way at a trade fair. I'd been booked to do an afternoon of tea leaf reading for some high-flying executives. Nahla showed up and acted like she had no idea she wasn't supposed to be there. She came with free samples, treats, and offering discounted readings. I was shoved in the corner, and she was given all the glory."

"That must have been frustrating."

"The first time it happened, I wrote it off as a mistake. But then she kept showing up and pushing me out of the way. I was losing business and money.

I was worried I'd have to give up my trade and do something else. Retrain and start from scratch."

"So you went after Nahla to persuade her not to keep treading on your territory?"

Petra leaned back in her seat and sighed. "Maybe I got too angry. We were fierce rivals and hated each other. Sure, she pretended she liked everyone, but she only loved money and fame. And I take back what I said."

"What was that?" Cythera asked.

"I'm not sorry Nahla is dead. Whether it was an accident or someone did it deliberately, I'm glad she's gone. Her snooty agent always said I was the one trying to ruin Nahla, but it was the other way around. Nahla almost destroyed my career, yet everyone was always on her side. They saw her as this golden girl who could do no wrong, and the more I protested, the more I was seen as the troublemaker."

"So you went after her again?"

"I had to! No one was listening to me. I bagged this major gig in Casino Village. Three months in a luxury casino, all-expenses-paid, for four hours of work a night. I was thrilled to finally land on my feet."

"Then Nahla showed up?" Cythera asked.

Petra nodded, a scowl on her face. "The first night I was there, she set up this all singing, all dancing event. There were fireworks, gifts, and prizes. Everyone flooded to her room to get their free readings. How can you compete with free?"

"Maybe it wasn't Nahla organizing these surprise appearances but her agent," I said to Zandra. "Amy was on the ball when we were at the bookstore. She was working non-stop, sending messages and marching around looking like she knew what she was doing."

"Petra sounds jealous," Zandra said. "She wanted what Nahla had, and when she couldn't get it, she killed her."

"I'm glad you've come around to the idea this wasn't an accident and that Sorcha wasn't involved," I said.

"Accident or jealous enemy getting rid of a problem. Whatever is going on, it shouldn't matter to us."

"It wouldn't, but for the fact, Sorcha is also a suspect and Nahla died in Vorana's bookstore. We need to make sure our friends don't get unfairly tangled in this situation."

Zandra sank into the seat and refused to look at me.

"Why are you questioning me about my problems with Nahla?" A flicker of uncertainty crossed Petra's face as if she was putting the pieces together. "I've never lied about disliking her, and everyone knows our history, but I wouldn't be so stupid as to blast into this town and kill her. If I wanted her dead, I'd do it somewhere quiet and out of the way. And I'd make sure no one ever found the body."

"She has a point," Zandra said.

"But Petra has a temper," I said. "She wanted to hurt Nahla when she came to the tearoom."

"Then she should get a better aim," Zandra said. "That teapot missed Nahla's head by inches. It was a rookie throw."

"It was the throw of a woman who'd lost control and wanted to cause damage."

"We need to ensure nothing's been missed during this investigation," Cythera said, drawing our attention back to the interview. "Unfortunately, there was contamination at the scene where Nahla was found, so we're uncertain if there was a struggle before she fell into the cauldron."

"What kind of contamination? Surely, whoever messed with that scene is the person you should speak to," Petra said.

Cythera shifted in her seat, and for a second, I thought she was about to glare at me, but she remained professional. "Questions have been raised about the exact cause of death, so everything needs to be looked into. And given your troublesome history with Nahla, we needed to speak to you."

Petra pressed her lips together then nodded. "I understand. And I'll answer any questions you have. You can see from the restraining orders that I was never violent. I yelled at Nahla and threw things, but never physically attacked her. I wanted her to stop jinxing my future. If she had, I would have had no problem with her."

"Petra must see she's got a solid motive for murder," I said. "Nahla was an obstacle she was unable to get around. She tried all different ways to succeed in the business, and every time, she was blocked by the same person."

"She wanted to be queen of the tea leaves," Zandra said. "If her blends taste as good as Nahla's, I'm happy to switch sides."

"Stop thinking about tea," I said. "It's not that delicious. Besides, you've always preferred strong coffee to give you that early morning buzz."

"Times are changing," Zandra said. "I plan on making lots of changes in my life."

I wanted to ask exactly what they were, but Cythera continued to question Petra, so I needed to focus. They went round in circles several times, covering the same ground. Petra stuck to her story, admitting she had a deep loathing for Nahla, and she was glad she was gone, but Nahla's murder had nothing to do with her. And although Petra seemed anxious, she wasn't panicked. She was paying attention, engaged in the questions, and there was no sign of nervousness or fear-induced sweating. If Petra killed Nahla, she was excellent at covering up the truth.

"It would be helpful if you could tell me where you were when Nahla died," Cythera said. "If you were with someone that night, it will clear your name."

"Clear my name? So you really are thinking it was murder?" Petra asked.

"As I said, we're covering all possibilities."

"You need to be more specific," Petra said after a second of hesitation. "I got to Crimson Cove late that evening and sought out Nahla as soon as I arrived. I found her in a cute tearoom with a load of other people. Everyone was around her, adoring her as always, and I saw red. I barged in, threw a teapot at her head, yelled for a bit, and then left."

"What did you do after that?" Cythera asked.

"I walked around to cool off. I knew I needed to change tactics, find a way to make Nahla think we could work together, so my business wouldn't be ruined and she didn't keep stealing what belonged to me."

"Did you come up with any solution to that problem?"

"Yeah, she killed her," Zandra said with a smirk.

"Nothing I hadn't tried before," Petra said. "I was planning on leaving. I didn't have anywhere to stay, and I knew I'd get nowhere with Nahla. I was walking away, when I saw a group of people come out of a bookstore. Nahla was with them. I followed, and they all went their separate ways. One of them went to a café, which she opened. A short while later, a few vampires wandered in."

I stiffened in my seat. Petra was talking about Sorcha's café.

"We know the place," Cythera said. "Did you go inside?"

"Yeah. I needed a sit down and something sweet to take the edge off my mess up with Nahla. The owner, I think her name was Sorcha, she was happy to see me. Well, she was to begin with. We had a small falling out. Anyway, I had some tea blends with me, so I invited her to join me since it was quiet. We brewed tea, talked about the town, normal stuff. Then I left."

"What time was that?" Cythera asked, her wings quivering. This was worrying. She thought she'd found a link to Sorcha being involved in Nahla's death.

"It was late. I was there until the early hours of the morning. Sorcha said she kept the café open late a couple of nights a week to cater to her vampire clients. I must have left around three in the morning. I went straight home."

"If that timeline checks out, Petra is innocent," I said. "I went back to the bookstore after midnight, but it was much earlier than three AM when I found Nahla's body. Petra couldn't have killed Nahla if she was in Sorcha's café."

Zandra lifted one shoulder. "Unless they're covering for each other, and they killed Nahla together."

Chapter 9

Surprise ally

"Hurry! Hurry! And stop dragging your feet. This is important." I bounded ahead of Zandra, turning and looking over my shoulder repeatedly. "What's up with you? We must speak to Sorcha to see if she's been interviewed by Cythera."

After Petra's interview earlier that day, where she'd revealed bonding with Sorcha over tea and chat, Cythera would be thinking just like Zandra; Sorcha and Petra had hatched an illogically awful plan to murder Nahla together.

"I'm tired. I knew work would be awful today, and I was right. I almost got bitten three times," Zandra said.

"Because you weren't paying attention. You spent most of the time looking at your mobile snow globe and eating snacks." It was most unlike my witch not to focus at work. She didn't love the admin, but she generally enjoyed her job. Today, she'd acted like it was the last place she wanted to be.

"Can't we do this another time?" Zandra whined.

"Time is of the essence. We must talk to Sorcha to see if she was with Petra the night Nahla died."

"Why do we have to be the ones to do it?" Zandra stopped to shake a stone out of her boot. "The angels have everything under control. They'll figure out if they were together and then charge them."

"Sorcha needs our support." I shook my head as I continued toward the café. Zandra had bugged me all day. Everything I said, she argued the opposite. She forgot to buy me lunch, and she'd left baguette crumbs in my comfy van bed.

Maybe Zandra no longer cared about Sorcha, but I did. She was a good friend, and I needed to warn her the angels were on the warpath. I slowed as I reached the café. The door was shut, and the lights were off. The place was empty.

"I knew this would be a waste of time," Zandra said. "She's already shut for the evening."

"Sorcha's been staying open late to boost trade." I pressed a paw against the glass. There was no movement inside.

"Maybe Cythera has already taken her in for questioning," Zandra said. "We're too late to do anything. Good. Let's go grab food."

"Only because you were so slow leaving work," I said. "It took you half an hour to change your clothes, when it usually takes two minutes."

"I'm lacking motivation. If we find Sorcha on our way, we can ask her to leave with us before she's charged with murder. Make a run for it while she's got the chance."

I turned and stared up at Zandra. "Where are we going?"

"I've been looking around, seeing what's out there. The job market is booming."

"You can't be serious. You've found your passion working with animals."

"I don't want to work with them if they keep trying to bite me," Zandra said. "And I'm always the one who gets covered in their excretions. Never you."

"I've been splattered with gross excretions a fair few times," I said. "If that's what's bothering you, Barney will buy you protective gear."

"It's not that. But I've been looking at some of the help wanted ads. There's good money to be made in the silver mines." Zandra turned away from the café.

"If you think working at animal control gets you grubby, wait until you go into a mine," I said. "And you don't have mining skills."

"Mining magic can't be that difficult to master," she said. "And you're always telling me I underestimate my abilities, so I'll pick it up in the blink of an eye. Anyway, if not the mines, I saw a want ad for an outward-bound instructor. You know, taking people into the wilderness and teaching them survival skills. It sounded cool. You get your own lodge, too. That would be handy, since we've been slumming it in Vorana's basement all this time."

"That basement is perfect. There's not a hint of slum about it." Worry swirled in my stomach. Zandra sounded serious about this move. But she couldn't be. Was this an elaborate hoax, and I was missing the funny side?

"I'll keep looking, but something perfect will show up soon," Zandra said. "And if we get to Sorcha before the angels charge her, she can slip away with us and be in the clear."

"We haven't made any decisions about leaving. And Sorcha is innocent, so she doesn't need to slip away anywhere. What's gotten into you?"

Zandra didn't even look at me. "I don't want to get too set in my ways."

I stamped a paw. "We're going nowhere. Especially not when Sorcha is in the middle of a possible murder. It's unfair to her. We always look out for our friends."

"We've done our bit. We showed up to give her a warning, but she's not here. It's time to move on." Zandra kept walking. "How about we find dinner?"

"No. We're going to Angel Force. We need to see what they have planned for Sorcha." I didn't bother to see if Zandra followed me as I stomped away. Talk of moving to a new job was unsettling. We had the perfect job at animal control. It felt amazing to help people with their magical critters and familiars when they were struggling. We kept Crimson Cove safe. And we had everything we wanted and needed here.

Maybe Zandra had taken a knock to the head when we tackled one of the feisty creatures today. It was the only explanation I could come up with to make sense of her strange behavior and desire to leave.

I didn't look back until I reached Angel Force. Zandra trudged behind me sullenly, her hands shoved into her pockets and her head down. I walked inside the building and was delighted to see Sorcha talking to Bertoli.

I dashed over and joined them. "Greetings! I've just come from your café. I was worried when you weren't there. How are things going?"

Sorcha clutched a mug, her hands shaking. "I've been better. I feel so guilty, even though I've done nothing wrong."

I glanced at Bertoli. "I take it you've been interviewed?"

Sorcha nodded. "I didn't do it! And I was so surprised when Cythera told me her theory."

"It's a ridiculous theory," I said.

Bertoli cleared his throat. "Cythera never has ridiculous theories. We received reports about how unfriendly Sorcha's been with Verity. It's possible she figured out a way to murder Nahla and then planned to implicate Verity in the crime."

"As I keep telling Cythera, I had no plans to frame anyone for anything," Sorcha said. "I was too busy worrying about how to keep my café going to plot a murder and then plant clues to frame somebody else for it."

"What about the kittens you're looking after?" I asked. "Did they see you go to bed after Petra left the café?"

"It was a vampire evening, so I always tuck any tiny kittens out of the way. The vampires find them a temptation. The kittens have their own room at the back because they're tricky to handle when they're in bad moods. I had two fires in my apartment thanks to them, so it's not safe to sleep in the same room."

"Then they can't alibi for you?" I asked.

"I don't need an alibi," Sorcha said. "I did nothing wrong."

"Of course. I'm just seeing how we can easily prove your innocence. What about your vampire customers?"

"There were only two of them there by the time Petra left," Sorcha said. "They were in the private room at the back because they had business to talk about and didn't want to be disturbed."

"Which means they were unable to confirm if Petra and Sorcha left at any point during that evening," Bertoli said.

"I didn't kill Nahla on my own or with Petra's help!" Sorcha's tone was shrill with panic. "This has nothing to do with me."

"Since you aren't behind bars, the angels know they're in the wrong," I said.

Bertoli spluttered a few words but fell into silence when I glowered at him.

Sorcha sipped her tea and grimaced. "I got this blend from Vorana. It's supposed to help calm you. It has all kinds of weird herbs in it. I'm not sure it's helping, though."

"I'll convince Cythera to see sense," I said. "We all know you and love you. No one thinks you're involved."

Zandra finally strolled into the office. She ignored Sorcha's greeting and headed to the kitchen.

"I was angry with Verity for messing up my comfy little business," Sorcha said, her gaze following Zandra. "I said mean things about Verity, and I regret that. And now I've gotten to know her, she's not so bad. I'm even considering getting involved in the tea festival. Although I suppose that won't go ahead now Nahla is dead."

"Which I'm sorry to say gives you a motive," Bertoli said. "By killing Nahla, the event is scuppered, and Verity could be discredited. That would be to your advantage."

"Bertoli, shame on you," I said. "You're a regular customer at Sorcha's café and her friend. She's only ever sweet to you. How could you even think such a dastardly thing about her?"

His cheeks flushed, but his gaze remained resolute. "I'm only doing my job. This is a working theory."

"It's a foolish theory. Has your job revealed concrete evidence Nahla didn't simply fall into her cauldron?" I asked.

He glanced at Cythera's office. She sat in there with the door closed. "We got the preliminary autopsy results back. There's bruising on Nahla's lower legs that suggests she was held under whilst in the cauldron. We think someone shoved her in and then prevented her from getting out."

"That's unfortunate," I murmured.

"But that person wasn't me," Sorcha said.

"It absolutely wasn't. Give me a few minutes. I'll speak to Cythera, and we'll figure this out," I said.

I ignored Bertoli's warning not to disturb Cythera. I checked if Zandra wanted to be involved, but she was busy sorting through a cookie tin someone had left in the kitchen. She'd be no use to me anyway, in the mood she was in. I headed to Cythera's office and tapped loudly with my paws.

A few seconds later, the door was opened. Cythera peered out, looking both ways.

"Down here," I said. "As well you know."

Her gaze lowered, and she scowled. "I don't want to be disturbed. I'm very busy."

I barged past her. "Yes, very busy and very important. But this won't wait. I need to ensure Sorcha is in the clear for Nahla's murder."

"Did I invite you into my domain?"

"I'm here now, so let's not make this trickier than it needs to be." I hopped onto Cythera's desk and settled on a pile of papers. They had a delicious crunchy feel under my toe beans. "Sorcha is innocent."

Cythera closed the door and grumbled under her breath as she returned to her seat on the other side of the desk. "Let's hear it."

"I'm glad you're letting me speak."

"You never give me any other choice but to hear all the clever thoughts bouncing around that fluffy head," Cythera said. "Be quick and then go away."

"Sorcha is a pillar of the community. She loves helping people. Yes, she has her concerns about Verity and the impact her teashop is having on the café, but she's not sly. She wouldn't be involved in a murder or in any attempt to frame someone else for that murder."

"Not so long ago, Sorcha was under the influence of a dark magic user. He had her convinced she was in love with him. He used toxic and dangerous magic on her. Some of that magic could have lingered and corrupted her."

"Nonsense. Sorcha didn't do this."

Cythera sighed and leaned back in her seat. "I agree with you."

I was so surprised, I almost fell off the desk.

"Don't look so shocked. I know how to run a solid investigation."

"What have you found out?" I asked.

"That it's impossible to keep you out of business that has nothing to do with you."

"I'm sticking around until Sorcha is in the clear, so you may as well tell me everything, or I'll set up home in that delightful looking cardboard box in the corner of the room and refuse to leave."

Cythera glowered at me then gave a curt nod. "On the night of the murder, Petra went into Sorcha's café with some of her tea leaf reading blends. They sat together and sampled a few cups."

"Just as Petra told us," I said.

"Yes, but she left something out of her initial statement. Petra was overheard insulting Sorcha."

"Insulting her about what?"

"Everything. She insulted her food, the café, and her outfit."

"It seems Petra is perpetually in a bad mood," I said. "Why would she be so mean to sweet Sorcha?"

"I couldn't tell you. Some people are born grumpy."

"You must know how that feels."

"What did you say?"

"Nothing. This is good news, isn't it? If Petra and Sorcha fell out, they'd never work together to commit a murder."

"Again, as much as I hate to, I agree. The vampires in the back room overheard the argument. Sorcha demanded Petra leave, and she said she'd be happy to go, and I quote: 'leave this rat-infested place with its burnt scones and sad-faced owner and never come back.'"

"Sorcha has never burned a scone in her life. What time did the fight happen?"

"The vampires were unsure. It was late. We can't get a definite timeline. Of course, since I've discovered Petra's been concealing things, she could also have lied about going to Sorcha's café as soon as she opened the doors. Maybe Petra watched the group leave the bookstore and grabbed Nahla the second she was on her own. She yanked her back inside and drowned her."

"It fits with the time I discovered Nahla's body," I said. "But surely, whoever did this would have gotten brewed tea on them. Did Sorcha mention Petra's clothing was stained? As you can see, my once glorious fur is still recovering from being dunked in the cauldron."

"No, and that's a problem I've yet to solve. Sorcha doesn't remember Petra looking wet or smelling strange."

"Maybe she had a change of clothes. Are you now pursuing Petra as the prime suspect?"

"We intend to talk to her again, but she's not making it easy," Cythera said. "She hasn't returned a single message I've left her."

"That's a sign of guilt," I said. "We have our prime suspect."

"Wrong. *I* have another suspect to consider. You have nothing. Go bother your witch rather than pester me. And stop shedding fur on my papers."

I looked through the glass partition. Zandra sat at Bertoli's desk, staring at his computer. "Have you noticed anything strange about Zandra recently?"

"When isn't she strange?"

"That's not nice."

Cythera half-smiled. "She's probably worried about her mother's upcoming wedding. It's one of the most stressful things you can ever do. I should know."

"Maybe it's that. She told me she wants to leave Crimson Cove," I said.

"Are you leaving us?" Cythera asked.

"No! I'm happy here, and so is Zandra. But for some reason, she's having a meltdown."

"That's a pity," Cythera said. "Once you go, I'll have a quiet life."

"A quiet life and a lousy conviction record."

Cythera grunted.

"I'm happy to be of service," I said. "But while we wait for Petra to resurface, let's question the other suspects."

"What other suspects?"

I gave her the cat version of a smile. "You see, you do need me around."

Chapter 10

Team cat

After convincing Cythera how indispensable I was, we'd agreed to meet later, once she'd arranged for us to speak to Nahla's husband, Ivan. I'd left her office to find Zandra gone.

Bertoli had no idea where she was, and a check back at animal control showed she hadn't been called in to deal with an emergency.

I hurried home, eager to update Zandra and get her involved in this investigation. Perhaps this was what she needed. She was feeling underappreciated and overworked. I'd get her focused on one of the things she loved: ensuring the bad guys got exactly what they deserved. When she was back in the swing of things, she'd forget this nonsense about changing careers and moving away from Crimson Cove.

When I got inside the house, it felt silent, as if the air hadn't been disturbed for some time. A quick dash around showed every room was empty. Zandra wasn't lounging in the basement, and there were no signs of Vorana or Sage. Perhaps they'd gotten over their dislike of dead body energy and returned to the bookstore to clear up. I was disappointed. I'd hoped a good poke around in a murder mystery would liven Zandra up.

A quick catnap, a few borrowed bites of kibble from Sage's bowl in the kitchen, and I headed back outside to find my witch. As I passed Angel Force, Cythera was walking out.

"Where are you headed?" I asked.

"Somewhere."

"How helpful. I hope you weren't thinking about going anywhere important without me," I said.

"The thought crossed my mind, but you're impossible to evade."

"And temporary partners never evade each other," I said. "Remember, this branch of Angel Force would be nothing without me. You said it yourself."

"I'd never say anything so ridiculous. Let's move. Ivan has agreed to speak to us. We're meeting him at the hotel."

"How did he sound when you spoke?" I trotted along beside Cythera, having to keep up a speedy pace since she made such big, purposeful strides.

"Surprisingly mellow, considering his wife just died."

"Most husbands would be blubbering wrecks after losing the love of their life. Should we be suspicious of him?"

"I'm suspicious of everybody."

"Not your trusty partner, surely?"

Cythera flicked a wing at me. "What little patience I have vanished around noon, so be on your best behavior, or this will end badly for you."

"My behavior is always impeccable," I said. "Where are we going?"

"The Sleepy Stardust Sanctuary. It's the best boutique hotel in Crimson Cove, so it was easy to figure out that was where Nahla and her entourage were staying."

"Zandra assumed they'd be there."

"Where is she? Are you two still fighting?"

"We never fight. She's just busy."

Cythera glanced down at me and arched an eyebrow. "You mean to say you've lost track of your witch?"

"My witch is free to come and go as she pleases. We normally do everything together, but we have our own lives. She's just choosing a different path at the moment."

"You always investigate together." Cythera was silent for a few seconds. "It's strange seeing you around town without her tagging along."

"You can be my temporary sidekick. You'll never fill Zandra's glorious boots, but you'll do."

Cythera rolled her eyes and kept marching. We arrived at the Sleepy Stardust Sanctuary a few moments later. The owner, Lizzie Briar, a petite half elf with adorable pointed ears and short green hair, was waiting by the entrance, her hands clasped together.

"Ivan and Nahla requested the honeymoon suite," she said after a brief greeting.

"Where is Ivan now?" Cythera asked.

"He's been keeping to his room after what happened to his wife. It's such an awful business. People are saying someone pushed her into a cauldron of hot tea." Lizzie led us through the hotel lobby.

"You shouldn't listen to gossip," Cythera said.

"It's not true?"

"It's true," I said. "And we're investigating who wanted Nahla dead. Has anything strange gone on in Nahla's party since they checked in?"

Cythera tutted at me but gestured for Lizzie to answer my question.

"They've been fine as guests. Amy is demanding, but I think that's because she wants everything perfect. She insisted on a certain type of bread and tea. No generic blends. She also goes through a lot of towels. But the requests are nothing unusual."

"Any fights?" Cythera asked.

"No problems like that. They haven't been staying long. I'd be happy to have them back again."

"Where is the honeymoon suite?" Cythera asked.

"Top of the stairs and walk to the end of the corridor," Lizzie said. "Room number sixteen."

We thanked her for the information and headed up the stairs.

"Don't get too excited about this interview," Cythera said. "It's more to cover bases. I don't consider Ivan a serious suspect."

"I won't. I'm still focused on Petra," I said. "But until she resurfaces, our paws are tied. And there's no harm in questioning Ivan. It's often someone close to the victim who does them wrong. For all we know, he could have gotten bored with Nahla.

Or become jealous of her success. Some men find it hard to accept not being the breadwinner in a relationship."

"Old-fashioned jerks," Cythera muttered.

"I'm sure that's not the case with your marvelous Maverick," I said. "He must delight in having such a successful and ambitious wife."

Cythera grunted a reply as she strode along the plushly carpeted corridor.

"There's no need to be coy. You bagged yourself a dream husband. He's always looking out for your best interests."

"He's a satisfactory husband. I could have been saddled with worse."

"High praise indeed. There's the room."

Cythera knocked at the door, and a few seconds later, a sleepy-looking Ivan pulled it open. He held a mug in one hand as he gestured us inside. His shirt was unbuttoned, revealing a fine set of abs. Nahla had been a lucky woman.

"Would anyone like tea?" Ivan ambled to an antique table with a kettle and mugs sitting on it. He heaped herbs into his mug and poured hot water over them. "I've got all the blends. Only the best for my Nahla. These help with anxiety. As you can imagine, I'm having a tough time dealing with everything."

"I'm sorry for your loss," Cythera said. "But no tea for me."

Ivan glanced at me, and I shook my head.

We settled into comfortably padded armchairs around an ornate open fire, and Ivan looked at us expectantly. "Have you made progress in finding out what happened? The last time we spoke, you were concerned about Petra's involvement."

"Petra is still a person of interest," Cythera said. "Given she arrived in Crimson Cove and immediately attacked your wife, we have to take that seriously."

"Of course. Of course. They had a difficult relationship. I think it boiled down to jealousy." Ivan inhaled the steam coming out of his mug, and his pupils dilated. Those were some powerful herbs. "I never had a problem with Petra, but I could tell she was fiercely covetous of Nahla's talents. Some people have an innate ability with their gifts, while others have to work to develop it. Petra isn't a natural tea leaf reader. She was rejected from the Academy five times before she gained her diploma to work."

"What about Nahla?" I asked.

"She breezed through the first time. Came out top of the class, so clever."

I tilted my head. "You don't seem sad your wife is gone."

"Nahla's not gone," Ivan said.

I glanced at Cythera, who looked as surprised as I felt. "I'm not sure I understand."

He inhaled the steam from his mug again, a lazy smile crossing his face. "There's no such thing as death. We're all made of energy. Everything is energy. From the chairs we sit in to the clothes we wear. Each and every one of us is made of vibrational energy. And we all know that energy can never be destroyed. It only changes form. That's a science fact."

"You're saying Nahla's not dead, she's just changed form?" I asked.

Ivan nodded. "Exactly! And what's wonderful about that is it means we all live forever. Of course, I'll never see Nahla in the form she was when we married, but it's comforting to know her energy has morphed into something else. She's still out there. She won't be aware of who she once was or what she did with her tea leaf talent, but she's not dead, just different."

"You don't have a wife anymore," Cythera said. "That must be hard."

"She's not in any form I'd ever be able to pick out in a crowd," Ivan said, "but isn't it a delicious thought? Everybody you've lost isn't lost, just changed. Whether it's your husband, a beloved familiar, or your favorite unicorn. They're all out there, just altered."

"Whatever gets you through this," Cythera said, sounding more than a touch confused. "Did you have a happy marriage?"

Ivan's face lit up. "Blissful. I felt like the luckiest man alive when Nahla chose me. She was a stunning older woman but an absolute firecracker in her youth. She dazzled everyone she met. She had men chasing after her all the time, even after we got married."

"How did you meet?" I asked.

"At a tea leaf reading conference. I was selling pestle and mortars for grinding herbs. Nahla was looking at the produce, and we struck up a conversation. I almost didn't invite her to lunch because I was so enchanted by her and didn't think

I stood a chance, but I took a risk, and it paid off. Less than a year later, we were married. Happiest day of my life. And I'd wake feeling grateful every day."

"How long were you married?" I asked.

"Twenty years. For some, that would be torture, but Nahla's work meant there was never a chance to get set in our ways or lose interest in each other. We were always traveling, planning events, or testing new tea samples. I was her guinea pig when she wanted to perfect a new blend."

"The herbs you're inhaling are from Nahla's supplies?" I asked.

"They are. Nahla made blends specific to the person when they requested a reading," Ivan said. "If she was doing a large event, she'd use a generic blend, but that meant her predictions weren't so accurate. But when someone paid for an hour of her time, she'd get their details and figure out exactly the blend of tea that would give them the perfect reading. This one was for an anxious client. People are often anxious if they're a first-timer, so Nahla wanted to calm them and ensure their nerves didn't affect the reading. I discovered it in her chest over there." He pointed to a large chest that looked like it should contain gold doubloons rather than dried tea. "Nahla took that chest everywhere with her, so she'd always have the herbs to make the right blend. She was so exacting about her work."

Although Ivan's lack of tears was unusual, if he genuinely believed his wife's energy was simply drifting around somewhere else, I could understand why he wasn't heartbroken. People had so many beliefs about what happened after death, so why should I doubt what he was telling us? It could be comforting to consider anyone you'd lost was just out there somewhere. Not dead, just a different energetic form.

"Where were you when you learned about your wife's death?" Cythera asked.

"I was here when I received a message. Apparently, you'd been trying to get hold of me on my mobile snow globe after Nahla was discovered, but I'm a heavy sleeper, and I never hear it buzz at night. And I usually have the thing switched off. Anyway, I was alerted by the charming lady who runs this place." A sheepish smile crossed his face. "I'm almost embarrassed to admit, I enjoyed a few too many mugs of sleepy time tea, and it knocked me out. I got told off by a guest the next morning for snoring so loudly. That was one thing that bothered Nahla. If I sleep on my back, I snore like a warthog."

"Didn't you think it was strange when she didn't come back to the hotel?" I asked.

"She did!" Ivan swirled the contents of his mug. "But Nahla adored her work. And she did her best work at night, so she was often up much later than me. After we left the bookstore, we returned here, but Nahla stayed up. I was tired, so I had my tea and turned in."

"Did she disturb you when she came to bed?"

"I don't think she did. Come to bed. When Nahla got an idea in her head, she'd often walk it out. She must have gone for a walk through the town, and that's when she was grabbed." His bottom lip appeared before he sank most of his mug of herbs.

"When was the last time you saw her?" I asked.

"In this room. I kissed her goodnight, and that was it."

"Did you hear her leave?"

Ivan raised his mug. "Thanks to these herbs, I was out for the count."

"Other than Petra, can you think of anyone else who wanted to harm Nahla?" Cythera asked.

Ivan slowly shook his head. "The whole thing is a tragic mystery. Petra was always ambitious, but I never thought she'd go this far. She's the only one who ever really had it in for Nahla. Some people's personalities clash, and this was an extreme example. I hope she's sorry for what she's done."

After a few more questions, it was clear Ivan had been under the influence of a powerful sedative tea, so he missed all useful information to pin down a timeline or learn if anyone visited Nahla at the hotel or if she left alone.

We thanked him for his time and left him with his pungent mug of herbs.

"We should check Ivan's alibi, just in case," I said.

"There's no motive," Cythera said. "He adored Nahla. She gave him a life of luxury. If he killed her, he'd lose that."

"Unless he inherits all the luxury. And as you like to say, we should cover all bases."

Cythera huffed out her annoyance at me but stopped at the reception desk, where Lizzie stood. "You were here when we contacted the hotel about Nahla. Did you take the message to Ivan?"

"Yes. I headed straight to his room to let him know you needed to speak to him."

"Did you see Nahla leave that night?" I asked.

Lizzie shook her head. "I thought they were all in their rooms. Ivan, Nahla, Amy, and Griffin came back together. I didn't see or hear anyone leave. Sorry, I know that's unhelpful. I was listening to a podcast out the back."

"What about when you delivered the message to Ivan?" I asked. "Did you hear anything unusual when you got there?"

"Oh! You mean his snoring?" Lizzie smiled. "Unfortunately, there were several complaints about the noise. When I got to his bedroom, I could hear him snoring through the door, so I understood the guests' annoyance. I would have said something, but given what had just happened to his wife, I didn't want to upset him. I knocked loudly and pushed the note with your contact information on it under the door."

"You see," Cythera said to me. "That was a waste of time."

"Not a waste of time. Discounting a suspect is only ever helpful." I thanked Lizzie, and we left the hotel.

Cythera was looking at her mobile snow globe, tutting to herself.

"Is there a problem?" I asked.

"Still no word from Petra. My angels can't find her."

I glanced up at the slowly lowering sun. "Keep looking for Petra. We'll speak to everyone else tomorrow."

"Everyone else?" Cythera tucked away her mobile snow globe. "Don't think this is a partnership. You're not clinging to me for companionship because Zandra has abandoned you."

"My dear Cythera, you make for an enjoyable companion, but I'll always have my wonderful witch to rely upon. Until tomorrow."

Chapter 11

Hissy witchy

After yesterday's adventure with Cythera, I'd returned home and was happy to find everyone there. I'd told Zandra about interviewing Ivan, but she barely paid me any attention, preferring to sit with Vorana as they munched their way through a family-sized box of deluxe truffles Vorana had picked up.

My witch finally passed out in a sugar coma around midnight, but I was up bright and early, eager to continue the investigation.

I jumped on her belly several times and licked her cheek until my tongue hurt, but she refused to stir. I stomped up the basement stairs and kicked open the door. Zandra would have to get up soon, or we'd be late for work. I marched into Vorana's living room, activated the snow globe that sat on the side table, and contacted Cythera.

Her face appeared on the globe. "What do you want?"

"Greetings and good morning to you too," I said. "What are we doing today?"

"I'm working."

"What time should I get there?"

"When hell freezes over."

"Did you fall out of the wrong side of the bed again?"

"Go away."

"I can be there in twenty minutes."

Cythera wrinkled her nose. "Is Zandra still giving you the cold shoulder?"

"My delectable witch is slumbering, and I want to get a head start on the day. We have to go into animal control, and that'll be busy, but I'll make time for you."

Cythera snorted. "That's kind of you."

"Is there any sign of Petra?"

"Frustratingly, she's still in the wind."

"That suggests she's guilty of something," I said. "I was thinking we should speak to Nahla's assistant, Griffin. He's been working with her a long time, so he'll know all the inside gossip."

Cythera's expression soured. "Unfortunately, we're sharing the same thoughts. I've arranged for Griffin to come into Angel Force at lunchtime."

"I'm having such an excellent influence on you," I said. "I'll be there at noon. I'll bring Zandra."

"There's no need. I have everything under control."

"Of that, I have no doubt. But I'm here to aid and oblige with a successful result. We'll see you at lunchtime." After saying goodbye, I hopped off the couch and returned to the basement. Zandra was finally stirring.

I leapt onto the bed and made biscuits on her belly with my murder mittens until she grunted and told me to get off.

"You need to be at work in forty-five minutes," I said. "And I've already made us exciting plans for lunch."

"Cancel them. I'll be too tired to do anything." She rolled onto her side, preventing my biscuit-making fun.

"We have a new suspect to question. Cythera has arranged for Griffin to visit Angel Force. She's demanding we be there."

"Of course she did. How many times has she told you to get lost this morning?"

"As if Cythera would be so rude. She has excellent angel manners." I waited for Zandra to respond, but she appeared to have dozed off.

I gently dug my claws into her bare arm until she jerked awake. "I'm worried about you."

"Focus on yourself. That's what you usually do."

"That's mean. Are you concerned about your mother's upcoming wedding? I understand they can be stressful."

"I don't care about that, and I'm not stressed about it. The last time I spoke to her, she was keeping things simple. They've fixed the date, the food was ordered, and they were working out how many people they want to attend. It'll be small and simple. Stress free and out of my hair."

"So why are you being so... Offhand with me?"

"It's called being relaxed. I'm not sticking my nose into other people's business. It feels good. You should try it."

"It's so satisfying to explore other people's business," I said. "And since someone was murdered in Vorana's bookstore, you must be slightly interested in whodunnit."

"I can't say I am." Zandra finally rolled out of bed and smacked her lips together. "I feel like I have a hangover."

"Too much chocolate," I said. "You have a puffy face, too."

Zandra shrugged as she ambled off into the bathroom and shut the door, preventing us from continuing the conversation.

Ten minutes later, we were upstairs, and Vorana presented us with a large pile of warm scones. "Fresh out of the oven. Honey tea scones. I bought a blend of special spices the last time I saw Verity. They're delicious. I'm about to eat my fourth."

"Where's the salmon?" I whispered to Sage from my seat.

"I'm still waiting. I haven't seen it come out of the fridge yet."

"We can't be expected to eat scones."

"They seem preoccupied with the treats," she murmured. "We'll give them a moment before we mention the lack of food on our plates. Vorana's been stuffing her face all night. She even snuck down here and ate three slices of cake. It's unlike her."

"She's having cravings? You don't think..."

Sage hissed at me. "Never! She'd be more sensible than to have a baby with Brodie."

"He's rough around the edges, but he has a certain appeal."

"Not at the moment he doesn't. He's been away for almost a week."

"On Angel Force business," I said. "It's good he takes his work seriously. Speaking of work, we're going to Angel Force at lunchtime."

"Haven't you solved that case yet?" Vorana reached for another scone.

"We have a prime suspect, but she's vanished," I said. "The angels are interviewing Nahla's assistant today to get the inside scoop."

"And apparently, we're needed." Zandra rolled her eyes. "Although I can't think why."

"Because we find clues that get overlooked and identify suspects the angels don't consider," I said. "It won't take us long."

"I remember Nahla's assistant," Vorana said. "Griffin. He seemed nervous. Lots of energy."

"I didn't speak to him much," I said. "But he'll know if there was trouble in Nahla's life. Perhaps he overheard her arguing with someone in the party she brought to Crimson Cove."

"Why don't we do the angels a favor and dig out Petra from wherever she's hiding?" Zandra asked. "You always have to make everything so complicated by speaking to everyone."

"Try a location spell if you think that'll help," I said. "But I'm sure the angels have tried it and gotten nowhere. If they had, she'd already be back at Angel Force."

Zandra pursed her lips. "They're making extra work for themselves and us. What a surprise. Bureaucracy at its finest."

Vorana nodded along with Zandra, seeming to agree that helping the angels was a terrible idea. Considering Nahla's body was found upside down in a cauldron in her store, I was astonished by her lackadaisical attitude.

"I'll let you know how it goes later," I said to Sage.

"If I'm still here. I may have perished from lack of food by then. Still no sign of any salmon."

I looked back at Vorana and Zandra, but they were stuffing their faces and making noises of pleasure. For some strange reason, we'd been forgotten about.

With an empty belly and a heavy heart, I left for work with Zandra. There was dried kibble in the office, and there were supplies for the critters we looked after at animal control, so I wouldn't go hungry. Sage, on the other hand, may have to do with eating honey tea scones. She'd do it for Vorana, but she wouldn't be happy about it.

Once we were at work, it was all systems go, and I barely had time to think, let alone worry about why Zandra was behaving strangely. There were six cases to investigate and no time for any rest until it was almost noon.

Zandra was just picking up a new file after unloading the latest captured critter when I jumped onto her lap.

I leaned against her chest. "If we don't go to Angel Force now, we'll miss the interview."

"So we miss it. Cythera will be thrilled we're not there."

I dug my claws hard into her knee and made her yelp. "I'll go on my own."

"Then go. I'll see you later."

I stared up at Zandra in shock. But there was no time to argue. I wanted to hear what Griffin had to say. "You're sure?"

Zandra lifted me off her lap and placed me on the floor. "Get out of here. You're being annoying."

I stalked out of the office. Had I done something to offend Zandra? Was she really so unhappy that she wanted to change all aspects of her life, including having me as her familiar? I couldn't bear such a thought. When we had a moment to ourselves, I'd confront her and get to the bottom of this problem.

I hurried into Angel Force just behind Griffin, and after quickly greeting Bertoli, we walked into the interview room, where Cythera was settling Griffin at a table. Griffin perched on the edge of his seat, his hands gripping the arms.

"There's nothing to worry about," Cythera said. "As you can imagine, we want to find out what happened to Nahla."

"Yes! So do I. I can't stop thinking about it. I haven't slept." From his ragged appearance and the bags under his eyes, he was telling the truth.

"Could you tell us how long you worked for Nahla in your role as her personal assistant?" Cythera asked after she'd run through the usual formalities and introduced me and Bertoli.

"Almost two decades. It was a huge promotion when she took me on. I'd been working for my former employer for five years, but my heart wasn't in it. Nahla was just finding her feet and making a name for herself in the world of tea leaf reading when a spot opened up to be her personal assistant. I went for the interview, and we clicked. I've been with her ever since."

"Do you like your work?"

"Very much. I shall miss it terribly. Nahla was hugely successful, and I enjoyed traveling with her. Some of her events could be fun, too. She worked her team hard but rewarded us well, and we got plenty of time off."

"That's good to hear. So many people don't like their work," I said.

"Not me. I can't imagine doing anything else," Griffin said.

"I'd like to know your thoughts on Petra," Cythera said. "As I understand it, there was a long-standing feud between Petra and Nahla."

"Oh, yes. Petra would get angry when Nahla got the jobs she wanted. But Nahla was the better tea leaf reader. She could probably read tea leaves in her sleep. She was so amazing at it. She charged a premium for her services, but it was worthwhile."

"Do you think Petra was involved in what happened to Nahla?" Cythera asked.

"Oh! I'm not sure." Griffin rubbed his chin. "They've bickered for as long as I've been working for Nahla. Surely, if Petra was going to do something to Nahla, she'd have done it a long time ago. Why pick now?"

"Had they had a particularly vicious argument recently?" Cythera asked. "Or did Nahla do something to offend Petra? Perhaps she secured a booking for a job Petra wanted."

"No, nothing like that. In fact, it's been a couple of months since I've even seen Petra," Griffin said. "The last few big events we attended, she wasn't there. I wondered if she'd hung up her cup and was no longer giving readings. It can be a ruthless business."

"Petra confronted Nahla in the teashop. She called her a liar," I said. "Why would she think that?"

Griffin shook his head. "Petra always said Nahla wasn't as good as she claimed she was at tea leaf reading. She thought her team, including me, did background work on clients so she could give unnaturally accurate readings."

"Is that true?" Cythera asked.

"Nahla never asked me to do anything like that. I was there to support her personal needs. I made sure her life ran smoothly so she could focus on her work."

"What about Amy? Or Ivan?" I asked. "Did they gather client information?"

"No, Ivan came along to support Nahla as her husband. He got a small salary from the business, but Nahla just liked having him around, so she kept him close. It was money he could spend how he liked and not work for it. Amy was in charge of the promotions and all the bookings. She wouldn't have time to root around and find background information on clients. We had so many, it would have been at least two full-time jobs. Nahla was a legitimate tea leaf reader. A superstar."

"You seemed surprised when we mentioned Petra as a murder suspect," I said. "You don't think she was involved?"

He fiddled with his thumbnail for a second. "I was thinking it could be Verity."

"Verity didn't like Nahla?" I asked.

"Nahla said a few unkind things about Verity's scones in an article. Tea and scones, you see, they go together so perfectly. Nahla sampled Verity's scones at a trade fair, and they were bad. She described them as stale and bitter. The quote got published in a lot of places."

I flicked an ear. "Is that a good enough reason for Verity to kill Nahla?"

"Well, Nahla was influential. Perhaps Verity was worried her business would suffer if the quote kept being circulated. She's expanding her tearooms into new towns, so bad press was the last thing she'd have wanted."

It wasn't a great motive, but at least there was a reason why Verity would want to harm Nahla.

"Could you confirm where you were the night Nahla was discovered?" Cythera asked.

Griffin startled and almost fell off his seat. "I'm not involved. Why would I want my employer dead? She was wonderful to me."

"It's just to rule you out of our investigation."

He grumbled to himself as he pulled a mobile snow globe out of his pocket. "Read my messages. I was dealing with a complicated booking that involved half a dozen agencies. We were chatting for two hours, and it needed my full attention. I was in my room at the hotel during the meeting. I had no opportunity to sneak off and hurt Nahla. I'd never want to hurt her. She took a chance on me. I had so much to thank her for."

"Do you often take meetings so late?" I asked.

"It's not unusual. We're a global name, so we need to accommodate different time zones. And Nahla was a night owl, so I adjusted to meet her needs."

Cythera took a few moments to scroll through the messages before handing the mobile snow globe back to Griffin. "Thank you. I appreciate that."

Griffin sighed. "I've been with Nahla for such a long time. I'm not sure what I'll do with myself."

"Perhaps Amy can help," I said. "If she works with other talent, someone may need a personal assistant."

"It won't be the same. I feel adrift on a sea of lukewarm tea, and tepid tea is always unpleasant."

After a few more questions, Cythera wound up the interview, and Bertoli showed Griffin out.

"I don't see Griffin as a suspect," I said to her. "He was nervous but helpful. And he clearly liked his job. By killing Nahla, he's left himself unemployed."

"There's no motive," Cythera said. "It's interesting he brought up Verity, though. I've heard no mention of a disagreement between Verity and Nahla."

"That's something else we need to investigate," I said. "And don't bother protesting. You love that I'm involved."

Cythera jabbed me with a wing. "I need food."

"I'll come with you. We can discuss our next target. Maybe Amy?"

"I prefer to eat alone."

"No, you don't. What are we having?"

"I'm not buying you lunch!"

"It could be my treat."

"How do you ever pay for anything? You have no pockets to keep money."

"My charm and flexible tabs. Zandra always settles my bills," I said. "How about the bakery?"

Cythera was complaining that I was being too clingy, when a haze of pale smoke appeared, and Amy Firebrand breezed into the office.

She waved away the smoke with a sharp smile. "My ears were ringing, so I know you've been talking about me. Shall we get this over with?"

Chapter 12

Wanna be famous?

"Have you hidden a recording device inside my station?" Cythera's wings curved outward, displaying her annoyance.

Amy arched an immaculately groomed eyebrow. "This is my first visit to this station or this town. When would I have had an opportunity to bug the place?"

Cythera fluttered her wings some more. "Then how did you know we were talking about you?"

Amy tapped the side of her head. "I'm mildly telepathic. An ability I inherited from a long dead dragon ancestor. I always know when I'm being gossiped about. And just to be clear, I despise it."

I hopped onto the desk closest to Amy. "Greetings! In truth, we weren't idly gossiping, but we were discussing talking to you about what happened to Nahla."

"I've already been talked to. I told the angels everything I know." She cocked her head. "I recognize you from the bookstore. You were with that dark-haired witch that didn't smile much."

"That's the most perfect witch in the world, Zandra Crypt. I'm her familiar, Juno."

"Crypt. Connected to the witches in Willow Tree Falls?" Amy's eyes lit with interest.

"The very same. It's a long and torrid tale of entanglement and affairs that, if you're interested, I'll entertain you with another time."

Amy whipped out a card and set it on the desk in front of me. "I've always wanted to represent a Crypt witch. You hear tales about them everywhere you go. They must have incredible stories about their demon fighting. I'm seeing it now, a reality series following the adventures of the Crypt witches. We could do specials where they go demon hunting. They could take us on a tour of the prison beneath their cemetery. And we could do an old-timer tales special with the family's wise women."

I flicked my tail, failing to mask a chuckle. "They're a private family. I'm sure they won't want that kind of notoriety."

"Everyone says that, but once they get a taste of fame, it changes them. And, of course, all the money and merchandising opportunities are impossible to resist. Sweat shirts. Coffee mugs. Cosmetics. Maybe a line in demon hunting equipment for the die-hards. How do you feel about having your face on a line of thermos flasks?"

"I'll mention it to them the next time we speak."

Cythera brusquely cleared her throat. "If you're done selling your services to the fluffy, we need to ask a few more questions about Nahla."

Amy held up a finger as her mobile snow globe buzzed. "One moment. I'm in the middle of a crucial negotiation. They're offering less than we agreed upon, and I won't have it. The warlock I represent, who shall remain nameless but is so handsome, he gets panties dropping at a hundred paces, has an incredible talent, and we won't be shortchanged." She tapped away on her mobile snow globe before looking up. "Proceed."

"Let's use an interview room," Cythera said.

Amy nodded, her gaze on her mobile snow globe. "Lead the way."

By the time we got into the room, she was muttering to herself as she sank into a seat. We waited for several minutes before she was finally done staring and tapping. "That should sort them out. So, what more can I tell you about Nahla?"

"Your work seems all-consuming," I said. "Have you been in the business long?"

"I've always been interested in celebrity," Amy said. "Ever since I was a child, bright lights and fame fascinated me. I briefly considered going into acting, but the reality is it's exhausting and boring. There's a lot of waiting around for scene changes, costume changes, or makeup re-touches. I've had fun working as an extra, but it put me off of being a full-time actor. Then I realized actors need representation. They're often so consumed by their craft that they're easy to take advantage of. That's where I step in."

Cythera took a breath to ask a question, but I jumped in again. "Do you specialize in representing any particular magic users?"

"Providing they have the talent, potential, and are flexible, I'm happy to work with anyone," Amy said. "I have every type of magic user, from witches to ogres, on my books. I even represent a few familiars if that's where these questions are leading."

"I've had my moment in the spotlight," I said. "It can be enjoyable, but you're always under scrutiny."

"Yes, you must learn to accept that a private life will no longer exist. One moment." Amy lifted her buzzing mobile snow globe and tapped away on it.

Cythera nudged me with an elbow. "Stick to what's relevant."

"I am. I'm getting the measure of her," I whispered.

"All done," Amy said. "I can only spare another five minutes. As you can imagine, Nahla's loss has left a giant hole in an extremely packed schedule. Even though she was winding down, I had bookings for her for the rest of the year."

"Nahla was retiring from tea leaf reading?" I asked.

"Yes, she'd been talking about it for a year. I have no talent with the leaves, but I understood how exhausting it was. After a large event, Nahla would sleep through two days straight. When she was younger, it wasn't a problem, but I'd been noticing signs she was struggling."

"That would have been bad for your bottom line," I said. "And it sounds like Nahla made you a lot of money."

"I won't deny that I've grown wealthy thanks to Nahla and her talents, but I always protect my artists. I never exploit them. Nahla wanted to step back to spend more time with her family, and I supported her."

"She wasn't fully retiring, though?" Cythera asked.

"No, Nahla was happy to honor the agreements we'd made. But we were talking about her getting an apprentice who she'd train to step into her shoes when she finally retired. We even interviewed a few people but had yet to find the right candidate." Amy briefly read a message that came in on her mobile snow globe. "Of course, Nahla's shoes were exquisite. No one would have filled them perfectly."

"Were any of the candidates unhappy about being rejected?" I asked.

"They were young, merely children." Amy smirked. "I just made myself sound old. But if you're suggesting one of them got revenge on Nahla because they didn't get a job, don't bother following that idea. I've put them in contact with other agencies, and they've all been successfully placed. There were no lingering grudges. As I said, I look after my own. You get a bad reputation in this business, and it's game over." She lifted a finger again and returned her attention to her mobile snow globe.

Cythera's hands flexed, and I could imagine her desire to wrench the thing out of Amy's hands and slam it into the wall.

"What would have happened if you couldn't find a replacement for Nahla?" I asked.

Amy finally looked up. "We were working on it. And I wasn't in a hurry. Of course, I never imagined this would happen. Occasionally, you get talent that can't handle the fame or squander their money on drink and drugs, but a murder is rare. Fortunately, I have another set of interviews planned. I'll push them up. I may be able to fill a few of Nahla's slots. Of course, the upcoming bookings will have to be canceled. It's a pity. Nahla was a well-loved expert. She'll be missed. I'll miss her, and I don't like most of the talent I represent."

Amy appeared genuine, but on the few occasions she'd met my gaze, her eyes were cold. She was saying the right things, but there was no emotion behind the words. She was like a business cyborg. This was just another business deal.

I decided to push more on her motive. From all accounts, Nahla made Amy a fortune, but if she'd wanted to step back from the business, that fortune would swiftly have dwindled to a trickle.

"May I ask how much money you made off of Nahla?"

Amy pursed her lips. "No, you may not. That's confidential information. And it's not relevant to this investigation."

"Perhaps it is," I said. "You admitted Nahla was soon to retire. The income from your partnership would have dried up."

Amy set down her mobile snow globe and met my gaze with an icy, level stare. "Although I won't provide actual figures of the income, let's just say Nahla made me a fortune. Why would I kill my golden goose?"

"Because she wanted to stop laying?"

Amy waved a hand in the air. "Nahla's death is a tragedy. And yes, in the short term, it represents a problem to fix. But the death of a star comes with positives. There'll be tributes, reruns of programs she was on, possibly a biography written. And there'll be the ongoing merchandising rights. I've negotiated terms on those that last for another ten years. When someone popular dies, everyone wants a piece of them. Whether that's a blend of tea they endorsed, a set of the crockery they put their name to, or a pin badge to put on their lapel. Death makes money. It may be morbid, but it's the truth. I've seen it several times with stars I've looked after."

Even when dead, Nahla was still a solid business opportunity for Amy. Perhaps she was worth more to her dead than alive, especially with semi-retirement looming.

"We're collecting alibis for everyone who was close to Nahla," Cythera said.

"And you want mine? I'm astonished you'd even consider me, but I suppose we all have jobs to do." Amy inspected her nails. "Six people can confirm we were talking about plans for a world tour of the old stars. When Nahla started mentioning retiring, I got this idea for a golden oldies tour. The fans love that sort of thing. They go mad to see faded stars come out again one last time. Something to do with reminiscing and remembering the good old days."

"Working so late?" I asked.

That now familiar smirk reappeared. "I love what I do. My career is my life. If I'm not working, I'm bored. Or sleeping."

"If you could provide a list of the people you were speaking to, we'll check the information now, and then you can be on your way," Cythera said.

After Amy had been provided with a pen and paper, she scribbled down the names, and Bertoli was sent off to check the details.

Amy leaned forward in her seat, her attention on Cythera. "For years, I've wanted to do a reality show at a branch of Angel Force. Is that something that would interest you?"

Cythera's brilliant blue eyes widened, and she froze in her seat.

"Don't dismiss the idea immediately," Amy said. "It would be a discreet crew of three. They wouldn't interfere in anyone's business, and all investigation details would be kept confidential. But it would be an exclusive, over-the-shoulder look into the complicated world of Angel Force. I've also been speaking to the angel training academy, and they're considering letting us follow cadets so we can see how you become experts in your field."

"I can't imagine that ever being approved," Cythera said.

"We've worked in busy departments before," Amy said. "We're discreet and efficient. You'd barely know the crew was here. I've been doing background research into this branch, and you get fascinating cases. I'm also intrigued by your use of freelance experts." Her gaze flicked to me.

"It's true. Cythera has the best freelance experts going," I said. "The conviction rate in town would be half what it is if it weren't for our unique involvement."

"I can imagine," Amy said, a small smile playing on her lips. "The pay is decent. There'd also be incredible merchandising rights. Imagine a line of angel merchandising. All white, of course. Maybe a sparkles line. And does one of your angels have pink wings? We can do a pink line, too."

"That would be Bertoli," I said. "He is delightfully pink-tinged."

"Stuffed toy cats for you, Juno. The kids would go wild for those. It would make you all very rich and disgustingly famous," Amy said. "What do you say?"

"I say law enforcement shouldn't be a source of entertainment," Cythera said sternly.

"Think about it. And give me a call when you change your mind." Amy returned to her mobile snow globe.

Bertoli reappeared a moment later. "I've spoken to three of the people on the list. They confirmed Amy attended a virtual meeting with them that evening."

"As if I'd lie to you," Amy said. "Now, I must go before this deal falls apart. Honestly, you think they'd be able to keep themselves under control for a few minutes, but no, if I'm not yelling at them, they're messing about like misbehaving imps."

"One final question before you leave," Cythera said.

"You've changed your mind about the deal?" Amy grinned. "Are you ready for me to make you a star?"

"Cythera already shines brightly," I said.

"I could make her even more radiant," Amy said. "What's your question?"

"Who do you think did this to Nahla?" Cythera asked.

"That's easy. It's got to be Verity."

"Not Petra?" I asked.

Amy scoffed a laugh. "Petra is a sweetheart."

"I've seen no evidence of sweetness," I said.

"Because you don't know her." Amy stood from her seat. "All you've witnessed is her veneer of sassiness. It's an act, put on for the media."

"It was a convincing act in the teashop," I said. "Petra aimed a teapot at Nahla's head."

"No, she didn't," Amy said. "That was an attention seeking bluff. I've gotten to know Petra over the years. Our paths cross because we go to the same events. Yes, she's spiky on the outside, but she's passionate about what she does."

"She was also passionate about her dislike of Nahla," Cythera said.

"Again, an act. You need an antagonist in every story, the bad girl who'll make the heroine look incredible."

"Petra didn't hate Nahla?" I asked.

"Hate is a strong word. Dislike, definitely. Jealousy? Perhaps. But spend time with Petra, and you'll see the real woman behind the mask."

"If we could, we would," Cythera said, "but she's vanished."

"She won't be far away," Amy said. "And she has no reason to hide. Focus on Verity. Scrape off that sugar frosting of 'OMG isn't the world amazing' and you'll find a vicious viper hiding among us."

Chapter 13

Wormy witches

I resisted the urge to tap the table with my paws as we waited for dinner to be served. It was later than usual, and after a day of grabbing snacks from the work supply store, I was more than ready for a hearty meal. Sage was of the same disposition, grumbling to herself and shifting in her seat at Vorana's kitchen table.

While we waited, Vorana, Zandra, and Sorcha stood around the stove, cooking together. It was a sight I'd never seen before. Zandra didn't know how to cook.

I glanced at Sage, and she wrinkled her booping snooter at me.

"What are they doing over there?" I whispered.

"Stirring up trouble. Vorana's been strange all day. Sort of floaty and not engaged with anything. She keeps forgetting about the bookstore, too. I reminded her several times that we needed to sort the wet floor and check the stock for damage, but all she wanted to do was bake scones and drink tea. It's as if she doesn't care about our business anymore."

"Here we are. Dinner is served." Vorana turned, revealing a huge glazed ham on a serving tray.

My mouth watered. That was more like it. With a full stomach, I'd be able to focus on Nahla's murder.

Everyone gathered around the table, and trays of vegetables, potatoes, and meat were passed around. I didn't wait until everyone's plate was full before tucking into the delicious-looking ham. I paused. It didn't taste right. Earthy and sweet.

"It's a new recipe." Vorana noticed me inspecting the meat. "I've never tried it before."

"It's interesting." I could barely swallow my mouthful. It was revolting. I glanced at Sage, and she was struggling, too. In fact, she spat her meat out and dropped it on the floor.

I tasted another piece, but it was just as weird. The meat wasn't spoiled, but it had such an unpleasant tang.

It seemed as if it was only Sage and me who noticed the problem with the food, since the others were tucking in.

With regret, I sat back in my seat. "We're making progress with Nahla's murder."

Sage nodded, but the rest of the dinner guests barely paid me any attention.

I persevered. "Surprisingly, the people we've questioned keep pointing to Verity."

That got Vorana's attention. "Not Verity. She's so sweet."

"Just like this ham," Sage said. "What did you do to it?"

"I'm experimenting. I got bored with my usual recipes. Eat up. There's plenty to go round," Vorana said.

Sage wasn't eating anything, and neither was I. The meat was nasty.

"I agree with Vorana," Sorcha said. "Now I've gotten past Verity's sugary sweetness, she's decent."

"That was a quick turnaround," I said. "A few days ago, you had nothing nice to say about her."

"I judged her too quickly," Sorcha said. "I like her. She gives away so many free samples."

"You were complaining about that."

"She is generous," Vorana said. "I got this recipe from her."

"Verity should stick to scone recipes," I said. "Savory dishes aren't her forte."

"I'll have your meat if you're not eating it." Zandra reached over and cleared my plate, tipping it onto hers. Up until that point, she'd barely spared me a glance since I'd returned from the interviews at Angel Force. She must still be angry with me for some unknown reason.

"Griffin and Amy suggested Verity killed Nahla," I persisted. "And it's interesting you mention sugar sweetness. Amy said if you scrape away Verity's veneer of nice, she's vicious. She warned us to watch out for her."

"I don't see it," Zandra said. "Maybe Amy and Griffin did it. They're pointing the finger at Verity to give themselves a chance to escape."

"Neither Griffin nor Amy have a decent motive," I said. "With Nahla dead, Griffin is out of work, and

Amy loses a client who made her a lot of money. And they both have alibis."

"There must be other reasons for killing Nahla." Vorana glanced at me. "You're usually good at figuring these things out."

"I'm excellent at it. And I'll continue to work on this case, although support would be appreciated." I looked at Zandra, but she was focused on her food.

Sage was trying the ham again but spat out her piece. She leaned over to me. "Vorana hasn't fed me all day. I had to eat half a dead bat I found outside because she didn't give me breakfast. And the rotting bat was nicer than whatever the heck this is."

I shook my head. It was strange for Vorana to serve such a terrible meal. Her food was always delicious.

"I don't care about the murder. Here, take a look at these job listings. I reckon I've got a chance with all of them." Zandra lifted a newspaper from the table and passed it to Vorana and Sorcha.

"You're still looking for another job?" I asked.

She nodded. "I told you, I'm done with animal control."

"Some of these sound interesting," Sorcha said. "You should go for it."

I hopped onto the table and looked at the listings. None of them were in Crimson Cove. "They're all out of town. We'd have to move."

"Trying something different is good for the soul," Vorana said. "We should all think about moving and getting new jobs."

Sage lurched in her seat, and if I hadn't dashed back and grabbed her by the scruff, she'd have tumbled to the floor.

"Did I hear right?" Sage whispered to me. "Vorana wants to leave Crimson Cove?"

"I'm sure she's just saying that to support Zandra," I murmured back. "For some reason, my witch has gotten it into her head that she wants to leave."

"Stop muttering, you two," Zandra said. "I haven't kept it a secret that I'm bored here. And no offense, Vorana, but I can't live in your basement for the rest of my life."

"Although you're welcome to stay for as long as you need, I could do with the extra storage. If I'm shutting the bookstore, I need somewhere to keep the stock until I sell it."

"Since when are we shutting the bookstore?" Sage asked. "That store was always your dream. You worked so hard to make it happen. You can't give it up."

"After Nahla died there, I'm not sure I want to go back," Vorana said. "She could be haunting the place."

"Ghosts have never bothered you," Sage said.

"They're good for business," I said. "Who doesn't love a haunted bookstore?"

"I don't want some creepy old spirit scaring me while I'm re-stacking books," Vorana said. "It can be somebody else's problem."

"What will we do if we don't sell books?" Sage's voice squeaked with panic.

"We could go traveling. I don't know. Zandra has the right idea, though. If she hadn't started talking about it, I'd still be thinking about inventory, repairs, and annoying customers. Now, I can be free."

"We can be free," Sage said. "I'm coming with you."

Vorana glanced at her. "We'll figure something out. Maybe you'd like a vacation from me, too."

"She doesn't want to be with me anymore?" Sage was panting, her eyes dilated.

"Calm yourself," I whispered. "There's something wrong here. I don't know what it is, but we'll get to the bottom of it. Zandra is just as bad. She's always interested in serving justice, but she doesn't care about Nahla's murder. And she's either ignoring me or being rude to me."

"I could sell the café," Sorcha said. "We could all go on an adventure together."

"You've got fire starting kitten duties. Now is the wrong time to be adventuring," I said.

Sorcha wrinkled her nose. "I'm sick of always putting myself last. Zandra's right. Things need shaking up."

My heart sank down to my perfect toe beans. Sage was equally anxious, shifting in her seat and gnawing on a front paw. When it became clear we'd get no replacement for the weird-tasting ham, I excused myself with Sage, got her settled in her harness, and we hurried out of the kitchen.

"What do we do?" Sage careened about in her harness, unable to stay still.

I stood in front of her to get her attention. "Something is making them behave like that.

Vorana would never leave Crimson Cove, and she'd never leave your bookstore."

"They barely notice us," Sage said. "Perhaps they've been enchanted. Or hexed. Cursed? Whatever it is, I hate it. I want to grab it and choke it until it slithers away and brings back Vorana and her love for all things bookish. Including me."

"Let's gather together the rest of the misfits," I said. "We need to know how widespread this is."

After making a number of calls using Vorana's snow globe in her living room, we headed out without bothering to tell anyone where we were going. In the mood they were in, they wouldn't care, anyway. Once we were outside in the moonlight, I cast a translocation spell that took me and Sage to Remus's estate. We appeared outside the main front door. I'd invited Archie, Binky, and Sammy. They were always out and about in town, so they'd know if anything strange was going on.

Archie and Binky were play fighting and almost knocked Sage over in their enthusiasm.

She hissed and batted each of them with a clawed paw. "Stop messing around. We have urgent business to deal with."

Sammy trotted over and greeted me by rubbing his head against mine. "What's going on?"

"I'll be quick, since you don't want to miss your curfew," I said.

"I'm fine for a short while. But I can't be out for much longer."

"Everybody, your attention please," I said. It took several more hisses from Sage before Archie and Binky stopped fighting and joined us.

I looked around the assembled group. "Something is wrong with Crimson Cove."

"You're wrong," Archie said.

I was startled by his blunt comment. "Could you elaborate?"

"Where should I start?" Archie stood and turned in a circle. "Your weird magic. Your nosiness."

"I'm a cat. We're supposed to be curious."

"Your grumpy witch."

"Take that back. Zandra is perfection."

"Not according to the gossip," Binky said. "You've been seen without her a lot recently. Familiars rarely leave their bonded magic user. It's not natural."

"You're here without Tia," I said.

"She's asleep. That's different."

"This early?"

"I may have cast a spell over her," Binky said. "Tia's been getting on my nerves. She keeps expecting me to help at the bakery. How boring is that?"

"You've always loved helping her," I said. "What's changed?"

"Too many weirdos getting into our business," Archie said with a growl.

My top lip curled. "You're referring to me?"

"Why do you always have to be so strange?" Archie paced back and forth. "Since you came to Crimson Cove, everything has been strange. People keep dying, magic keeps going funky, you keep bringing trouble to my vampire's door. Maybe the town is fine, but you're the problem."

Binky nodded. "If you weren't here, we'd have no troubles. We could get away with whatever we wanted to."

"What do you want to get away with?" I asked. "And I've always helped you. When the bakery burned down, I supported you. When Remus got himself in trouble with Angel Force, I defended him. More than once."

"Maybe you were the one to set fire to the bakery," Binky said.

"You know who did it! You're not making sense. These troubles are linked to Nahla's murder. But something is going on that's affecting the wider population."

"This has nothing to do with the clumsy witch who fell into her cauldron." Archie barked a laugh. "I couldn't believe it when I found you soaking wet on the bookstore floor. It was pathetic. Your magic didn't work, and you weren't strong enough to haul the body out. You'd given up. What kind of familiar does that make you?"

"I hadn't given up, but I did need help. As my friends, I assumed you'd be happy to offer that assistance." What was going on with Archie and Binky? They were being so strange. And Sammy was sitting quietly, watching the whole thing. He usually came to my defense whenever anyone said a bad word about me.

I drew in a deep breath. "I was going to ask if you'd seen anything in town that suggests other people are being affected. But having spent time with you, I see you're in trouble, too."

"It's not us. It's you!" Archie said. "If we run you out of town, the problems will vanish."

Sage hissed. "Leave Juno alone. I've witnessed this weirdness, too. Vorana's talking about leaving. She hadn't spoken a word about wanting to move until Nahla died in her store."

"That's the reason she wants out," Binky said. "If Tia found a body in her bread oven, she'd freak out."

"We should do it! Dig up a corpse to leave in the oven. It would be so funny to see her reaction," Archie said.

"You had better be joking," I said. "The bakery would have to shut for weeks while they dealt with the aftermath."

"More time off for me," Binky said. "I only see that as a bonus. What size of corpse should we go for?"

"Please, focus. If you're being affected, then your bonded magic users are in trouble, too. I assure you, I'm not behind this, but it has to do with Nahla's death. We must find out what happened to her. If her murder triggered something in Crimson Cove, we need to fix it before it goes too far."

"And before some idiot digs up a corpse and sticks it in a bread oven," Sage muttered.

"Let the town fall into chaos," Archie said. "My vampires are planning something big, that's all I care about. Not the death of one stupid witch."

"What is Remus planning?" I hadn't seen Remus for some time. Ever since he'd been involved with a curious vampire staking on his land, he'd withdrawn from town life. Although, if the effects of Nahla's murder were rippling across the community, it made sense he no longer wanted to be sociable. Everyone was behaving so out of character.

"We want to show the town what we're made of," Archie said. "The vampire hive feels defanged. It's embarrassing."

"Why?" I asked. "The vampire hive is well respected. Remus is popular."

"We have a point to prove," Archie said. "We won't be seen as weak."

"Nobody thinks you're weak," Sage said. "Tell your vampires to behave."

Archie snapped his teeth at Sage.

"That's enough!" I'd made a mistake by getting everyone together. I wanted to work as a unit and figure out this problem, but all I'd created was a rift.

"This is boring," Binky said. "Let's get out of here."

"We'll go to the cemetery," Archie said. "See if there are any fresh graves."

Before I could issue a warning, they bounded away, body slamming each other and filling the air with growls.

"I should go too," Sammy said. "I can't miss my curfew."

"How do you feel?" I turned to him and carefully studied him. "Any odd desires or dark thoughts?"

Sammy turned and walked away. "I feel that Archie and Binky are onto something."

I stared after him in wide-eyed shock. Sammy had been affected, too. It hurt my heart to see him so indifferent to me.

"This sucks," Sage said. "What a bunch of useless jerks."

I took a moment to compose myself. There was no help to be had from Zandra or her friends. My magical misfits were broken and seemed beyond repair. Only me and Sage were the same as always.

"These problems involve tea leaf rivalry," I said. "Everyone is saying Verity murdered Nahla, but what if the weirdness drifting through town is affecting the suspects, too? They're pointing to someone it couldn't possibly be, when there's a clear killer wandering among us."

"Petra? The mean one who likes throwing teapots?" Sage asked.

"She must be behind this. And she's hiding because she's guilty. Guilty of a lot worse than shoving Nahla into a cauldron." I stamped a paw. "She's messing with our precious town. We need to find Petra and stop her."

Chapter 14

Weedy shock

"We're doing everything we can to find Petra. Go bother somebody else." Cythera blocked our entrance into Angel Force. "And it's late. Why aren't you pestering your witch for treats? Still fighting?"

"We're working out one or two issues," I said tartly. "Zandra has more urgent things on her mind than hunting for Nahla's killer."

"Maybe she's finally come to her senses and has decided to get rid of you," Cythera said.

"You must be tired because you got the late shift, but there's no need to be rude," I said. "We're helping with this investigation. Don't you want Petra found?"

"My angels have looked everywhere, but she's vanished," Cythera said.

"Location spells?"

"Of course. We have friendly witches who help with that."

"What did their spells reveal?"

"Scatters. It's as if Petra is blowing in the wind. The magic doesn't settle on a single location."

"She could be blocking you," Sage said. "There are counter spells to location magic. If Petra doesn't want to be found because she thinks you're about to arrest her for murder, she could be casting a spell that makes her look like she's in more than one place at the same time."

"She must have powerful magic to fool our mighty angels," I murmured.

"You can flatter all you like, but you're still not getting in," Cythera said. "And we have other cases to focus on. Things always get busy at night. Ever since that business with Voss's weird pizza, people enjoy getting up to mischief as soon as the sun goes down."

"Isn't that what people have always done?" I asked.

"Not to this degree. It's pushing us to the edge. Of course, we want this murder solved, but you're making too many demands on my time. Come back in the morning. If Petra is hiding from us now, she'll still be hiding when the sun comes up." Cythera shooed us out of the station and slammed the door in our faces.

"You'd think the angels didn't want our help," Sage said. "I'd suggest we call it a night, but with all the strangeness going on at home, I'm happy to stay out late. I may even sleep in the yard when we get back. Vorana kept muttering in her sleep last night as she tossed and turned. She accidentally knocked me off the bed!"

"I'm happy to pull an all-nighter. We need to find Petra and figure out how everything's gotten so twisted up in these tea leaves. If she's the cause of this muddle, we'll make her pay."

Sage trundled along beside me in her harness. "The weirdness started before the tearoom opened and the fortune tellers came to town though, didn't it? All that strange business with the herbs getting mixed up on Voss's pizza and messing with supernaturals."

I nodded. "Voss and Roland swore blind they didn't make a mistake. That must have been what happened, though. There's no other explanation for how toxic mushrooms got on the wrong food."

"You're missing my point," Sage said. "Nahla's death didn't trigger the weirdness. Weird stuff was going on before then."

"Nahla's murder enhanced it," I said. "Before she died, Zandra and Vorana weren't talking about selling up and moving out of Crimson Cove."

Sage grunted. "That's true. Let's find Petra and see what she's doing to our witches."

"When Petra spoke to Angel Force, she said she was planning on returning home after confronting Verity, but perhaps she stuck around. We should try the Sleepy Stardust Sanctuary. If she was watching Nahla, she'd want to keep a close eye on her."

We changed direction and headed to the hotel. Once inside, we found Lizzie looking through menus. She looked up as we approached. "Checking in?" There was a playful smile on her lips.

"Still investigating what happened to Nahla," I said. "Did a guest called Petra Teaping book a room here recently?"

Lizzie hesitated. "Is this official Angel Force business?"

"They've got their hands full, so they called in the experts to get to the bottom of this mystery."

Sage grunted but played along.

Lizzie set down the menus and headed back to the reception area. "Petra did book a room, but I haven't seen her. Not all day. And when her room was cleaned, the bed hadn't been slept in. It was like nobody had been there."

"Did Petra even check-in?" I asked.

"The key isn't here, so she must have done," Lizzie said.

"How many nights has she booked in for?"

"Two. I didn't make the booking or hand over the key, so I don't know what her plans were while she was in town."

"She was here to cause trouble," Sage said.

"Could we look in her room?" I asked. "We urgently need to speak to Petra, so any clues she left behind could help us figure out where she went."

"You can take a quick peek, but I didn't see you do it." Lizzie grabbed the master key and led us up the stairs. "I don't want to get in trouble."

"We won't say a word about your assistance," I said. "And your help is much appreciated."

Lizzie opened the door, and we hurried inside. As she'd explained, the room appeared pristine, although there was a scarf lying on the back of a chair, which we gave a thorough sniff.

"Smells like honey," Sage said. "It's pungent. We should be able to track the scent if Petra's still in Crimson Cove."

With the smell fresh in our booping snooters, we thanked Lizzie and hurried out of the Sleepy Stardust Sanctuary. Once we were on the streets, we put our enhanced sniffing abilities to the test.

"I've got a faint whiff of something this way." Sage set off at a speedy trot, and I followed. She paused at the bookstore and stared with sad-eyed despair at the building where she'd spent so many happy hours.

"Vorana won't leave Crimson Cove," I said. "She loves this store. Your home. And she's enjoying herself with Brodie."

"I can be rough on the guy, but he's making an effort with me," Sage said. "He bought me chewy sticks and a catnip mouse the other day. He must have figured out that, if he gets on my good side, Vorana will want to keep him around."

"He's certainly put a smile on her face," I said. "I wish Zandra would smile more. Maybe I'm partly to blame for her dark mood."

Sage set off walking again, still convinced she'd picked up Petra's scent. "Why say that?"

"I'm always pushing her to be the best version of herself," I said. "Zandra's got such potential and power, but she doesn't always believe in herself. She's been better recently, but maybe I've pushed her too far. I never expected her to consider leaving all of this behind."

Sage continued sniffing and walking. "Could it be you?"

"That's what I said."

"No, not your pushing her to be the best version blah blah. You know, the dragon stone.

You got all your power back, so maybe Zandra is feeling something is different between you," Sage said. "Your bond is changing, and it's making her uncomfortable. After I got injured and lost the use of my legs, my bond with Vorana shifted. It took months before we were normal again. She felt guilty, and I felt too much anger. We figured things out, but the ride was rough."

I huffed out a breath. I'd thought the same thing myself more than once. Even though I hadn't activated the magic and absorbed it into me, it lingered in the basement, ready to be set free. "Our bond does feel different. Could it really be what's making her want to leave town?" I asked.

Sage bumped me with her harness. "If it is, it needs to stop, because it's messing with Vorana, too."

"It's not my intention to mess with anyone," I said. "But Crimson Cove feels like a tangled mess, and I'm not sure how to unpick the problem."

"It's always been spicy," Sage said. "Even before you and Zandra moved here, we had an abnormally high rate of weird goings-on. It's a powerful place, and sometimes that power gets perverted."

"I've perverted nothing," I said. "I may be immensely powerful, but I'm not reckless. Let's focus on the fortune tellers. They were the trigger. I think Petra saw red and ended her rivalry with Nahla for good. She wanted to become Queen Bee of Tea, and Nahla stood in her way."

Sage lifted her head and inhaled deeply. "I'm still getting that faint honey scent. But if we keep going in this direction, we'll end up on the pebble beach, and you know how much I hate that place."

"Your wheels always get stuck in the holes," I said. "Or you end up standing on a dead guy in a dark cave."

Sage shuddered. "I still have nightmares about finding that body. I thought it was a fish. An enormous slimy fish. But no! Someone dumped a body in the spot I planned to stand in. How selfish is that?"

"We may get diverted before we arrive at the beach. Keep tracking the scent. You clearly have a better nose than I do."

"I can hunt out a dropped treat from five hundred paces." Sage continued leading the way.

I tried a few times to pick up the scent Sage was convinced she'd discovered, but as we grew closer to the beach, I was overwhelmed with the smell of damp seaweed and salt-tinged air.

We got to the shoreline and stopped. Fortunately, the tide was way out, so there was only an expanse of damp pebbles and sand in front of us. Given how late it was, there was no one else on the beach, not even young revelers who could usually be found around impromptu campfires with a beer in hand.

"You're sure you've picked up the right scent?" I asked Sage.

"It's here. Try a location spell," she said. "If Petra is close, it'll be harder for her to mask her location."

I summoned a spell between my paws and threw it across the pebbles. It scattered and spun before landing in several locations and disappearing.

"She's still blocking us," Sage said. "Although I've never seen a location spell do that. It landed on six different spots on the beach. Usually, when someone blocks a location spell, it fizzles out to nothing."

"Let me try again." I focused hard and sent out the magic. The spell swirled around us before landing on the same six spots on the beach.

"It looks like it's working," Sage said, "but Petra can't be in six places at once. And if she was in one of the locations the spell landed on, we'd see her from here."

"We need to tread carefully," I said. "If she's able to break that spell, she must be even more powerful than I realized."

"If she's so powerful, why didn't she simply kick Nahla off the top spot and claim the tea leaf crown for herself? There's no need for murder. Killing someone will never get you what you want."

I scanned the beach for any sign of our elusive suspect. "According to Nahla's husband, Ivan, Petra struggled to learn the fine art of tea leaf reading. She barely made it through training."

"If you don't have a natural ability for that sort of thing, it'll always be a struggle," Sage said. "It would be like me training to be a rocket scientist. The lack of opposable thumbs would always have me at a disadvantage."

"That would be a problem." I conjured a location spell for the third time and cast it again. I focused on the largest red dot that landed on the pebbles. "Let's head that way. It's where the spell lands the strongest. Even if Petra's not here anymore, she could have dropped a personal item that'll give us a clue as to where she went."

Sage heaved herself onto the pebbles with much grumbling. She only took a few paw steps before she got wedged.

I hurried behind her and shoved her out of the hole. "Float! It's much easier when you do that."

"I'm tired!"

"It's a basic spell. Don't be grumpy and lazy. Use your magic."

Sage slid me a glare then threw magic over herself. She lifted a few inches off the pebbles so she was able to float beside me without getting snagged every few steps.

"Isn't that much better?" I said. "You avoid all the slippery pebbles and soggy seaweed under your paws. I'll never be a beach fan. And don't get me started on the sea. Cold, salty, and gross. You know, fish pee in there?"

Sage floated along, scanning the pebbles. "This is my least favorite place in the world. Apart from the vet's."

I grumbled an agreement.

"I'm getting a stronger scent," Sage said. "Petra must be close."

We were almost on top of the spot where part of the location spell had landed. I slowed and looked around. There were mounds of slippery seaweed around us, deposited as the tide went out. Most likely, there were crabs and starfish entangled in the pungent sea vegetable.

I sidled around several lumps before stopping by a particularly large one. I sent out the spell again, and it landed on top of the seaweed with a sparkling sizzle. "Sage, get over here."

She stopped sniffing a clump of seaweed and joined me. "What did you find?"

"Cast a light ball over this seaweed. There's something here."

A pale glow surrounded us, and I reluctantly sniffed the pile of damp, sticky muck, looking for whatever it was that kept triggering the location spell.

"I can say for certain Petra isn't here," Sage said. "We'd see her!"

I dug through the grotesque seaweed for several seconds before uncovering Petra's head.

Chapter 15

One or two?

"How did you know Petra's body was on the beach?" Cythera sounded irritated that I'd successfully done her job for her.

"Decades of experience and a superb companion who knows what she's doing." I nodded at Sage, who was grumpily crouched into a small ball since a chilly drizzle had started five minutes after we'd summoned Angel Force to assess our gruesome discovery.

"Did you get a tipoff that Petra was here?" Cythera directed several of her angels as they scoured the beach and continued finding the rest of Petra. The location spell indicated she'd been disassembled into six parts, so that's what they looked for. So far, we'd found the head, both arms, and one leg. The leg was marked with thin red whip lashes. Possibly from being entangled in the seaweed and dashed on the pebbles.

I inched closer to Cythera and attempted to hide under one of her large wings to escape getting soggy fur.

She ruthlessly batted me away. "Concentrate! I know you think this is a game, but I'll be the one filling in the reams of paperwork because of this disaster. What kind of monster would do this to Petra? How did you figure out she was here?"

"I assure you, it was as simple as following our booping snooters," I said. "We wondered if Petra decided to stay in Crimson Cove to resolve her issues with Nahla. Indeed, she did, and we picked up her scent and followed it here. My location spell discovered the rest. Well, I discovered Petra's head under that clump of seaweed. It gave me a fright. Did you notice the eyes were bulging?" I tried again to get under Cythera's wing. She had plenty going to spare, but I got smacked on the head and shoved away once more.

"Did you touch any of the body parts?" Cythera asked.

"I nudged the head with a paw when I first found it, but I'm happy never to linger around cooling limbs. I noticed neat slice marks, though. The cuts must have been achieved using magic. Or a scythe. Are we scheduled any visits from Death?"

Cythera tutted.

"Somebody meant business," Sage grumbled from her damp furry huddle.

"You definitely don't slice someone into six portions by accident," I replied. "But this leaves us with a problem."

"Just one?" Cythera grumbled.

"I was convinced Petra killed Nahla. But now Petra is dead, too. Did Petra kill Nahla and this was a revenge attack? Or does whoever killed Nahla have a list of people they're planning to slay? Is this the start of something more serious?"

"That's too soon to say," Cythera said.

"This was clearly a murder. And the evidence you've gathered from Nahla's body suggests the same," I said. "You should be alarmed in case a serial killer is picking off skilled tea leaf readers one by one."

"Why would they do that?" Cythera directed one of her angels over to another piece of Petra.

"Tea leaf readers predict the future," Sage said. "Maybe the killer doesn't want to know what their future holds."

"Petra told them anyway, and this is the result," I said.

"Or maybe the killer went to Nahla first, hated what they heard, so they killed her," Sage said. "Then they paid Petra for a reading and got the same information. Double death was the result."

Cythera's sharp gaze drifted across the beach. "It could be Verity. Everyone we talk to keeps suggesting she did it. Well, at least that she killed Nahla. Kill one tea leaf reader, why not two? Maybe she didn't like what she heard about her future."

"Where does Verity live?" I asked.

"She's renting a small house close to the teashop," Cythera said.

"Giving her time to sneak back to the bookstore and deal with Nahla. I'm still unsure why she did it, though. They were working together." I inched under a wing, since I was getting soggy. "What was Verity's alibi for the time of Nahla's murder?"

"She said she was at home, asleep," Cythera said. "She'd had a busy day."

"Was that verified?"

"No. But at the time, we had no reason to consider her a suspect in anything."

"We must now," I said. "Petra's actions suggested she was the killer, but maybe we got it wrong."

"The great Juno, admitting to a mistake?" Cythera smirked and deliberately folded her wings tight against her back, so I had no shelter. "I never thought I'd see the day."

"I always admit when I'm wrong, but I so rarely am that it is a novelty. Petra could still have done it," I said. "And what happened here suggests her killer was full of anger. This style of slaying looks like a punishment killing. Petra may not have died under the first chop."

"Not if they took the arms and legs first and left the head until last," Sage said.

"More wild theories," Cythera said. "We won't know anything until we've assessed the scene and examined what's left of Petra."

"While we're waiting for your most excellent angels to do that, we should visit Verity," I said. "Ask what she's been doing this evening. And prod her more about her alibi for Nahla's murder."

Cythera looked away. "I suppose you want to come along while I do that?"

"I'm honored you'd ask. It would be my pleasure to assist you."

"Do I have to come too?" Sage asked.

"You could stay here and get wet. Or go home. Maybe Vorana will be more receptive to finding you a tasty supper," I said.

Sage grunted. "I'll come with you. But then I'm finding a cozy spot in the yard and sleeping until noon. No one is to disturb me."

I was glad to have my curmudgeonly friend by my side. Cythera was being even curter than usual, so it was pleasing to have Sage and her familiar surliness as my sleuthing companion. I was used to her grumps. When everything else in Crimson Cove felt strange, I clung to every tiny piece of normalcy I could find.

Cythera provided me with Verity's address, and after barking orders at her angels to gather the rest of the evidence and take it back to Angel Force, she took to the wing and vanished.

"Cythera could have offered us a ride," Sage said. "We'll get soaked through if we walk."

"Hold on to me, I'll take us there." I cast a translocation spell, and we arrived outside Verity's quaint little house a second later. There was a cascade of dying roses winding up a trellis and over the top of the entrance. The garden was wild with different blooms and long grasses.

"This is good hunting ground," Sage said. "There are all sorts of critters hiding in there."

"We'll have to come back another time and investigate rodent treats for our witches," I said. "If Verity isn't arrested for murder, she'll welcome the pest control."

Cythera thumped down from the sky a second later, her wings splayed. She stood and shook her feathers back into order before striding to the door and whacking it.

"There's no need to alarm Verity," I said. "We need answers, not to scare her into silence."

"I'll handle this. If Verity has been giving us the runaround, what else can she expect but to feel my wrath?"

"You have wrath?"

"Don't push me, fluffy. It's late, I'm tired, and I have another body to deal with," Cythera said.

I glanced at Sage as Cythera whacked a fist against the door repeatedly.

"Coming! Coming! Hold on just a moment." Verity's high voice sounded on the other side of the door as the bolt slid back and she inched it open. "Oh! Sorry. I was asleep. Do you know what time it is?"

"Time you told us the truth." Cythera barged in, and we scurried in after her. I murmured an apology.

Verity hurried after Cythera, still tying her robe around her waist, her hair messy and her mascara smudged under her eyes. "What have I been untruthful about?"

"How much you disliked Petra." Cythera turned on her, and the fury in her eyes made me take a step back. She was really rattled by this case.

Verity swallowed, her face pale. "I feel like we've gotten off on the wrong foot. Would you like some sweet tea? It's my own blend. Very soothing."

"No tea," Cythera said. "Where have you been this evening?"

Verity blinked several times, and her gaze shifted to me and Sage. I gestured for her to answer the question before Cythera went apoplectic.

"Well, I... I had a quiet evening. I finished working at the teashop. We were busy all day. Then I had dinner, a bath, and an early night. Why do you want to know my movements?"

"Did you have a problem with Petra Teaping?"

"No! No problem." Verity chewed on her bottom lip. "She could be prickly, but we were always civil to each other. I'd often see her at trade shows. I'd be there to replenish stock or find new suppliers, and Petra would be buying tea for her readings. Sometimes, we were at events where we sold our services. There was no bad blood between us."

"Petra's dead," Cythera said.

I stared up at her in surprise. Cythera was never this blunt. She could be clumsy with her questioning, but this was unprofessional. Maybe she was hoping to see Verity's reaction by revealing the news so starkly. Or perhaps get a surprise confession.

Verity appeared frozen to the spot. Then she wheezed out a breath, sounding like a squeaky balloon, and collapsed into a chair, one hand over her heart. "Petra's dead? I thought... Nahla. Do you mean, Nahla?"

"Both of them are dead," Cythera said. "Now, do you want to tell the truth?"

"The truth about what?"

"Your hatred of Petra. And Nahla. Did you kill both of them?"

Verity shook her head, her gaze shifting to panic and fear. "No! This is awful. I'll admit, I wasn't on friendly terms with Petra. I saw how badly she treated Nahla over the years. I felt sorry for Nahla. She was a professional and an absolute genius with the tea leaves. Petra, on the other hand, could be spiteful and cold."

"Did you ever warn Petra to stay away from Nahla?" I asked.

"It wasn't my place. But if they ever had a set-to when we were at an event, I'd intervene. I'd usually take Nahla off somewhere and distract her with tea and scones. By the time we returned, Petra's anger had blown out, and we could carry on as normal."

"Do you think Petra murdered Nahla?" I asked.

"I... I really couldn't say. I don't want to think I've ever met a killer."

"What about the fight at your teashop?" I asked. "Petra was furious with Nahla."

"That was nothing. They'd fought before." Verity hesitated. "Petra did seem particularly angry, though. I always thought she was jealous of Nahla. Nahla was so personable and clever, and Petra was icy and sharp. She got passed over so many times for fortune telling jobs because she couldn't get along with people. Although..."

"Yes? What do you know?" Cythera asked.

"I don't know for certain, but I believe Petra has been signed for a massive promotional campaign. Her name and face could go nationwide. It'll make her the star she's always wanted to be. Oh! Well, it would have done if she were still alive."

"How did she secure such a prestigious gig?" I asked.

"Through Nahla's agent, I believe. I'm not sure if you're aware, but Nahla was considering semi-retiring. She wanted to spend more time with her family, including her sweet husband, who's been feeling terribly rejected," Verity said. "When Ivan married Nahla, he knew her career would always come first, but over the years, he's found it wearing. They'd been having disagreements, so Nahla agreed to cut back her hours. That left Amy looking for a replacement."

"And Petra was the replacement?" If this was true, it gave Petra the perfect motive. She killed the competition to reap the rewards.

"You'll have to confirm all of that with Amy," Verity said. "She was angry that Nahla was considering hanging up her tea leaf cup. I think she'd planned Nahla's career for the next decade, so when Nahla said she needed to focus on her family, it left Amy in a hole."

"Which she swiftly filled with Petra. Do you know if Amy had meetings with Petra to discuss her future?" They'd have needed to put plans in place before Petra was signed to anything, and that would have given her time to figure out how to wipe out Nahla and claim the tea glory.

"They must have gone through some form of negotiation," Verity said. "As far as I know, Petra has no representation, so she'd have needed to meet Amy to finalize any deal."

I looked at Cythera. Petra sounded guilty of murdering Nahla, but we were still left to figure out who killed Petra. She'd had a bright future ahead of her but was cut down before she could grab it.

"Why did several people bring up your name when I asked who they thought killed Nahla?" Cythera asked.

Verity's mouth dropped open. "That makes no sense. I just want to be friends with everybody. Who thinks I'm a killer?"

"We can't share those details with you," Cythera said. "But there have been claims you're not all you say you are. You use scones and saccharine to fool people."

Verity gulped. "For what purpose?"

I was interested in that answer, too. I wasn't sure where Cythera was going with this line of interrogation. After several seconds of silence, it seemed neither did Cythera, because she turned away and gestured for me to continue the questioning.

"Can anyone verify what you were doing this evening?" I asked.

Verity pressed her lips together. "I live alone. I like to keep my own space. Besides, this house is only big enough for one person. There's only one bedroom, and the kitchen is tiny. It works for me, though."

That meant she had no alibi and couldn't easily clear her name.

"Can you think of anyone who would want Petra dead?" I asked.

"Nahla, obviously. Although she never said she wanted Petra out of the way, she just wished she wasn't so angry all the time." Verity shrugged. "Of course, unless Nahla has returned as a vengeance ghoul, she can't be involved in Petra's death. She was definitely killed? It couldn't have been an accident?"

I flicked my tail. "It was no accident. Anybody else?"

Verity shook her head. "I'm sorry. I'm not being helpful. I'm in shock over the news that both Petra and Nahla are gone. It'll be a huge blow to the tea leaf community."

I looked at Cythera, who was glowering at Verity, but she didn't add anything useful to the discussion.

"Thank you for your time," I said. "We'll leave you to it."

Verity stood to show us out, but a thud overhead made me slow.

"I thought you said you lived alone?" I asked.

"That's my naughty cat. He's always knocking things over. Well, you'd know all about that." She hurried to the front door and opened it. "If I think of anything else, I'll let you know."

There was another thud. It was a sound way too big to have been made by a cat. Unless we were talking about a full-grown panther hiding up there.

I turned and bounded up the stairs.

"Wait! Don't go up there." Verity was close behind me. "The bedroom is messy. I haven't tidied in days. There's underwear on the floor!"

I shoved open the first door I came to. Nahla's husband, Ivan, lounged on the bed, wearing only his boxer shorts and a smile, an empty bottle of champagne rolling on the wooden floor next to him.

Chapter 16

Secrets revealed

Ivan blinked lazily at me. "Verity? I didn't know you could transmogrify."

I stepped closer and wrinkled my booping snooter. Ivan smelt funky. Sweet and sickly.

I was closely followed into the bedroom by Cythera and Sage. Verity remained in the doorway, a quivering mess, her mouth opening and closing as if attempting to find a rational explanation for this surprise guest. But no words would convince me there wasn't something untoward occurring between these two.

"You make a cute cat." Ivan chuckled to himself. "Come closer and let me stroke you."

"That's not me!" Verity's voice came out breathy with nerves, the words a rushed noise.

Ivan tilted his head and peered at me. "I just heard you speak like Verity."

"Look up!" Verity finally composed herself enough to form a sentence. "That's an actual cat. You've had too much champagne. You can't see straight."

His glassy gaze shifted upward, and his eyebrows lowered. "I'm confused. Who is who in this room? Why is that cat on wheels? And is this angel joining us for some fun?"

"Pull yourself together," Cythera snapped. "I'm an official member of Angel Force, and I'm investigating your late wife's murder. We've spoken several times. You must remember me."

For a second, Ivan's dopey expression morphed, but then a blanket of stupor enveloped him again. "Of course. We have? Yes! I remember now. I think. Oh dear. We've been caught with our actual pants down. Is it too late to run?"

"If you run, we'll think you're guilty of something," I said. "And you clearly are, since you're in Verity's bed."

"Find him something to wear," Cythera said to Verity. "I can see practically everything from here."

"Isn't it glorious?" Ivan lounged back on the bed, giving us an even finer display of his toned physique. "My darling wife insisted I look after myself. She gave me plenty of time to do so. I could spend hours in the gym every day if I wanted. And she always served me the most nutritionally complete meals. I wanted for nothing."

I sniffed one of his bare legs that dangled off the edge of the bed. "Sage, come here. Your nose is more finely attuned to complex smells than mine."

She trundled over and smelled his leg. "Weird. Kind of herby."

"And sweet, too," I said. "Is it a type of lotion?"

"The smell is seeping out of his pores." Sage wrinkled her booping snooter and backed away. "And have you noticed his eyes?"

Ivan was chuckling to himself again about nothing in particular, seeming completely unembarrassed that he'd been caught in Verity's bed after they'd recently rumpled the sheets. His pupils were hugely dilated, and his eyes were glassy.

Verity hurried into the room with a flowered robe, which she gave to Ivan. He fumbled around for several minutes before succeeding in getting his arms into it, but he left it open, so it was ineffective at concealing his goodies.

"I'm sorry I lied to you. I didn't mean for this to happen." Verity gestured at Ivan.

"You said you were alone this evening," Cythera said. "When we arrived, you said you'd been sleeping."

"Because I realized I'd made a horrible mistake." She gestured at Ivan again.

"Was it really so terrible?" Ivan managed to sit up in the bed and collected the empty champagne bottle off the floor. He inspected it, seeming hopeful that it may miraculously refill itself.

"You don't seem embarrassed to have been caught with another woman," I said to Ivan.

He looked up from the champagne bottle. "I haven't. Verity can't be my other woman because I don't have a woman. A wife. I mean, Nahla's out there somewhere, but I have no clue what energetic form she's taken. Not a form I could marry. We wouldn't know each other."

"Maybe she's now a venomous hornet the size of my head, and she'll fly by and sting you for getting busy with her friend," Sage muttered.

"You seem very comfortable in Verity's bed," I said. "How long has this been going on?"

"This was the first and last time," Verity said. "I've gotten to know Ivan over the years. He's a lovely man. We'd often bump into each other at events and share a drink and a laugh. But when Nahla was alive, we were only friends."

"You never shared a bed?" Cythera asked.

"No!"

"You'd have plenty of opportunity to carry on an affair behind Nahla's back every time your paths crossed," Cythera said.

"Never. I was close to Nahla," Verity said. "I'd never betray her friendship. I've been so busy setting up my franchise and opening stores that I haven't had time for a proper relationship. But I still have needs."

"And it appears Ivan filled them," I said.

"You can't blame a fellow. She's cracking looking. Who doesn't adore a woman who can bake? And let's not forget the things she can do with a jar of honey," Ivan said.

"Shush! They don't need the details." Verity's cheeks flamed with heat.

He shrugged. "Perhaps we were both lonely and seeking comfort. This is the first time I've lost a wife. It's not much fun to be widowed."

"We've really done nothing wrong," Verity said after a second of tense silence. "Yes, Ivan is recently widowed, and I've just lost a dear friend, but I'm sure Nahla wouldn't mind us finding comfort in each other's arms."

"Although you've broken no official laws, Nahla may have appreciated you waiting more than five minutes before jumping into bed with her husband," I said.

"She's not even cold!" Sage said.

"Body's cool within twenty-four hours of death," Cythera said.

"Even when boiled?" I asked.

Cythera flicked a wing at me. "Yes!"

Sage settled on the wooden floorboards and closed her eyes, not seeming convinced by that curt reply.

"Nahla was a good old thing," Ivan said. "But her work was her one true passion. She loved me as best she could, but it was lonely being married to her. She made it clear her career would always have priority, and usually, I didn't mind. But I sometimes felt like I'd been widowed a long time ago."

"And I noticed Ivan's struggles," Verity said. "That's how we became friendly. I'd see him sitting alone at an event and keep him company."

Ivan's smile was lopsided as he tipped up the empty champagne bottle. "Nahla would go off for weeks, and I'd have no idea where she was. It was the main reason I decided to travel with her. Even if she was off working, we'd be in the same town. But moving from place to place was tiring. I have simple needs, and one of them is my own bed to clamber into every night and familiar surroundings. Somewhere I feel safe and at home. You can't do that in a hotel room. You never know who has a master key and can sneak in."

"Nahla did her best, but she was obsessed with her tea leaves. Our friendship got neglected, too," Verity said. "I'm not proud of being found in this situation, but we've broken no laws."

I curled my gorgeous tail over my front paws and stared at the guilty-looking couple. Well, Verity looked guilty. Ivan just kept staring at the champagne bottle with hopeful desperation.

What if they'd been seeing each other on and off for some time? It gave them a motive for wanting Nahla dead. If they'd formed an attachment, they could have decided they wanted to be together and had to dispose of Nahla. She didn't want to let Ivan go, so he had no choice but to kill her.

Nahla would have trusted Ivan if he'd asked her to return to the bookstore with him. And she'd have turned her back on him when standing by the cauldron, making her an easy target.

But the same logic applied to Verity. They'd been friends, so if Verity suggested they go to the bookstore after everybody had left, Nahla wouldn't have considered it strange. Verity could have made an excuse and asked for Nahla's help.

"Since you lied about your alibi this evening," Cythera said to Verity, "let's try this again."

"Alibi for what?" Ivan asked. "You can't think Verity had anything to do with what happened to Nahla, can you? And that happened days ago. She doesn't need an alibi for tonight."

Verity caught hold of his hand. "They're not here about Nahla. It's Petra. She's dead."

"Two deaths?" A confused glaze slid over Ivan's face again. "Nahla and Petra are both dead?"

"Yes! I don't know what happened, but this angel and her companions showed up and questioned me about what I was doing this evening. Of course, I didn't say you were here because of how it would look to outsiders."

"Well, I was here." Ivan ran a hand down his face. "This is shocking. What kind of town are we staying in where people get bumped off all the time?"

"Crimson Cove is perfectly safe," I said.

"Not for my wife. And now Petra! She was difficult, but she always spoke her mind, and she didn't hide what she coveted. At least you knew where you stood with Petra. How did it happen?"

"We're not releasing that information at the moment," Cythera said. "But Petra's death is suspicious. We're speaking to everyone who had a connection to her to find out what happened."

"You can rule us out," Ivan said. "We've been together all evening. We've barely left this room. Neither of us is involved."

Verity nodded. "I only lied because I knew what you'd think of this situation. We got caught up in the moment. Blame the champagne if you like, but I think we were lonely and in need of company. And as your furry companion said, we've broken no law."

"These two aren't my companions," Cythera said.

"We're her expert consultants," I replied, "brought in to investigate cases when the angels grow flummoxed. They contact us at least once a week. Talk us through exactly what you did this evening from the time you left work. When did you meet Ivan?"

Verity drew in a slow breath. "I shut the tearoom at six, and Ivan was walking past. We talked for a moment, and he invited me for a drink. I said I wasn't in the mood to be sociable because I was tired. He said how about an alternative to partying in a crowd, and we could go back to mine, so I invited him over."

"With some champagne," Ivan said. "It was Nahla's favorite drink. She always received gifts from fans. You could guarantee at least one bottle of champers would be delivered to the house every day. She liked to bring some with her when she traveled. Since she's gone, and has no use for it, I decided we'd enjoy it instead. Raise a toast to Nahla."

I peered under the bed and saw another empty bottle of champagne. "It seems like you raised more than a glass in Nahla's memory."

Verity's cheeks flushed. "One minute, we were reminiscing, then we were joking with each other, and then we were kissing. It all happened so fast."

"Not too fast, I hope?" Ivan asked.

Verity patted his hand. "We really have been here all evening. Besides, even if we hadn't, we have no reason to harm Petra."

"You admitted you didn't like how she treated Nahla," I said.

"I did, but not enough to do anything like this. Petra sometimes let her passion bubble over, and that turned into anger, but I didn't wish her harm, and I never wished her dead."

"Petra was career-driven, just like Nahla," Ivan said. "I admired that. She was a funny old thing, but I had no problem with Petra, either. Most of these tea leaf types are quirkily obsessed with their abilities. And I should know, since I was married to one for such a long time."

"You admired the very thing that took your wife away from you all the time?" I asked.

Ivan chuckled. "I suppose so. Do we have any more bubbly?"

"You've drunk more than enough," Cythera said. "Has this been your plan all along?"

"Plan? I'm not one for making plans," Ivan said. "That was Nahla's department. Well, her team made all the decisions for me. For both of us, really. Even down to what we ate and the clothes we wore. They set my alarms, sorted my food, made my appointments. I could sit back and let it all happen. Didn't have to think about a thing."

"That must have felt stifling," I said. "Nahla and her team basically controlled you."

"I'm glad of it. If they hadn't controlled me, I'd be nowhere. I always was lazy. It irritated Nahla if I didn't stick to the agenda. Eventually, I had no choice but to do so or have Amy drag me where I was supposed to be. She's frightening. If someone crossed her, they wouldn't live to tell the tale. Now, there's a thought. Perhaps it was Amy who killed Petra?"

"Don't say things you can't prove," Verity said. "We really had nothing to do with what happened to Nahla or Petra. I'm still in shock over what happened to Nahla, and I'm stunned someone has been saying I was involved."

"You?" Ivan snorted a laugh. "I can't imagine a less likely killer."

"The best ones are always successful at hiding it," I said. "That's how they get away with their crimes for so long."

Verity's shaking hand slid up to her throat. "I promise, it wasn't me. Whoever is saying it was must have a taste of sour grapes. Maybe they're jealous of my success. If you tell me who they are, I'll speak to them and sort this out."

"That's not happening," Cythera said. "I'm bringing you both in for formal questioning."

Ivan jerked upright and shook his head. "That's a waste of time. We've both been here all evening, just like Verity said. And when my poor Nahla met her end, I was asleep at the hotel. I'm sure you've checked by now that I was in my room. I'm innocent of both crimes."

That was a problem. Ivan had been at the Sleepy Stardust Sanctuary when Nahla was murdered. And if he'd been here with Verity, he couldn't have been on the beach. It was possible they'd snuck out together to murder Petra, but the way Ivan slurred his words and how glassy his eyes were, I doubted he'd be able to stand, let alone masterfully slice a powerful magic user into six neat chunks and then hide them among the seaweed.

"I'm also not involved in either death," Verity said. "I was here with Ivan tonight, and in bed alone, asleep, when Nahla died."

"We met earlier that evening for a bit of slap and tickle, though, didn't we?" Ivan said. "That was the reason I slept so soundly."

"Slap and tickle?" I pounced on Ivan's error. "I thought this was the first time you'd been together?"

"Oh! Maybe slap and tickle means something different to you." Ivan looked at Verity for help, but she shook her head and sighed.

"We know exactly what it means," Cythera said. "I've heard enough. We're taking you in."

Chapter 17

Done deal?

"I'm going to Angel Force after breakfast to find out the latest." I prodded Zandra's knee to get her attention. Something that had been lacking since I'd returned home last night to update her about the investigation.

"Good. You do that." She grabbed two freshly made buttermilk pancakes and a scone and set them on her plate as she slouched at Vorana's kitchen table.

"You should join me. You've been out of the loop," I said. "It's been strange working with Cythera without you there to protect me."

"What do you need protecting from?"

"Cythera's surliness. Her inability to recognize my value. Her wings. She keeps hitting me with them. They're big and heavy, and she's not gentle. She also seems angrier than normal."

"You can look after yourself," Zandra said. "I've got three job applications I want to get in by the end of the day, so I've got no spare time."

My heart skittered. "You're really going through with it?"

"Of course. I'm done with this place."

"I'm coming with you, right?"

"You seem settled here. You could always stay with Sage."

My throat tightened, and I looked away.

Vorana breezed into the kitchen, minus Sage. "What are we talking about?"

"My new career," Zandra said at the same time as I said, "Murder."

Vorana wrinkled her nose. "You always have to chase the dark things, Juno. Why can't you be a normal cat?"

"That would be boring. Where's Sage?" I hadn't seen her since last night.

"She's here somewhere."

"She's always at the table waiting for breakfast," I said.

"I saw her digging a hole outside," Zandra said. "She was also looking at that old metal shed. The one where we kept Cinder."

"I miss that dragon." Vorana sighed. "She was a bundle of scaled trouble but so pretty."

"Less trouble than a cat with sass," Zandra muttered.

Vorana poured a fragrant tea for both of them and grabbed her own scone. Since it looked like I wasn't being served breakfast, I left the table and the gossip about new jobs and headed outside. There was no sign of Sage, but there were noises coming from the shed. I headed over and peered inside. Sage had set up a pile of old newspapers in one corner. She was lying on them.

"What are you doing?" I asked.

"I've moved out. I'm invisible to Vorana, so what's the point of sticking around?"

I stepped inside. The shed smelt of damp, and there were mouse droppings by the door. "She's caught up in Zandra's excitement about a new job. Once that blows over, she'll be back to normal. I'm sure this is just a phase. Maybe an early midlife crisis."

"I don't know what it is, but I hate it," Sage said. "When we came back last night, Vorana ignored me and wouldn't let me sleep on the bed. I laid on the carpet for a while, but then she almost stepped on me when she got up to go to the bathroom. Has someone covered me with invisibility magic?"

"I see you perfectly well. I'm sure Vorana can, too. Come inside. We'll hunt for breakfast in the pantry."

"That's another thing! Why has Vorana stopped feeding us? She always feeds us first. But I've had nothing sent my way. She doesn't want me anymore." Sage closed her eyes and deflated. "I knew this day would come."

"No day has come." I sniffed the pile of damp papers she was trying to turn into a bed. "This oddness has to do with the investigation."

"All they're interested in is eating scones and drinking that weird-smelling tea," Sage said. "If it's not that, they're talking about leaving Crimson Cove then their eyes go blank. It's like they've been programmed to only have two interests."

"They are oddly obsessed with new recipes and the pungent tea Verity's been selling," I said. "Could the tea be having an unexpected effect on them? It's making them pine for new beginnings or change."

Sage wheezed out a huff. "I smelled something like that on Ivan last night."

"The man bathes in champagne. That's what we smelled. It oozed from his pores."

Sage grunted. "I want things to go back to how they used to be."

"Then the sooner we go to Angel Force and see if Ivan and Verity have confessed to the killings, the better. When Verity is behind bars, she won't be able to provide any more of her tea. If that's making Vorana and Zandra act strangely, we'll soon know."

"I'm tired. I barely slept last night. I kept worrying I was going to be trodden on."

"We'll be an hour at the most. And Cythera won't want us lurking around Angel Force, so she'll give us the news and shoo us out. After we're done there, you can sleep for as long as you like."

After much sighing and grumbling, Sage got herself back into her harness, and we left the house. There was no point in saying goodbye to Vorana and Zandra.

"I was thinking about what we uncovered last night," I said as we headed onto the main street and toward Angel Force. "Verity killed Nahla to get Ivan all to herself. That's an obvious motive."

"Agreed," Sage said.

"How does Petra's murder fit in, though?"

"She could have found out about the affair."

"And threatened to expose them?"

"So they bumped her off together," Sage said.

"People have been saying to watch out for Verity, so perhaps she worked alone," I said. "Ivan seems too distracted to focus on something as messy as murder."

"Stoned off his gourd, you mean," Sage said. "That wasn't just champagne messing with him last night."

"He drinks a lot of Nahla's special blend teas," I said. "Maybe it should only be used when reading fortunes, but he drinks it like it's the regular stuff, so it messes with his head."

"Add in a whole bottle of champagne or two, and you're in trouble," Sage said.

"So, Verity worked alone," I said. "Nahla had what she wanted, and Ivan would never leave Nahla, since she provided him with a life of luxury and leisure, so Verity did something about it."

"What about Petra? If Verity was with Ivan that night, how could she have gone to the beach?"

"You said yourself, Ivan is high on life and herbs. He could have dozed off for half an hour, giving Verity the chance to slip out."

"To meet Petra at the beach? Did they arrange the meeting or did Verity accost her and take her there?"

"I can't see it being a formal plan," I said. "Verity must have found out where Petra was hiding and grabbed her when she had the chance. She magicked them to the beach, killed Petra, and scattered the body parts to confuse things. Maybe she hoped the tide would wash away the evidence."

"Maybe Petra's not been missing all this time," Sage said. "What if Petra confronted Verity about the affair, so Verity abducted her? She's been holding Petra prisoner and waiting for an opportunity to get rid of her. When she was with Ivan last night, he went to sleep, and it gave her a chance to have an alibi and the opportunity to kill Petra."

I nodded. "Case solved. Get a confession from them and put them behind bars. The teashop will have to shut if Verity's locked up, meaning an end to her scones and herbal teas that everyone is so obsessed by."

"And finally, we'll get our witches back." Sage stamped a paw. "Problem and case solved. I'll soon be sleeping on the bed again with a belly full of food."

It was a plan I endorsed.

We entered Angel Force. It seemed oddly quiet. It was early, but there were usually at least a half-dozen angels bumbling about. And Cythera was always in residence but not today.

Bertoli wandered out of the break room, a large cookie in one hand and a leaflet in the other.

"Greetings! Where is everybody?" I hurried over to him.

"Working. There are cookies. Help yourself if you want any. They're almost gone."

"We're good for cookies. What news about Verity and Ivan?" I hopped onto Bertoli's desk.

"They've been questioned." He dropped into his seat.

"Have they confessed?"

"Not yet. They keep saying they're innocent." He munched his cookie and looked at the leaflet he held.

"What have you got there?" I asked.

"It's about the new festival."

"The tea festival?"

"No, this one is all about mushrooms. Roland Moldsworth is organizing it. Every time I see him, he tells me about some new vendor or specialist who's coming to town to take part. It's supposed to be a big deal."

"After everything that happened at Voss's pizza parlor, they must have figured out that mushrooms aren't our friends," Sage said.

"Neither are tea leaves, given the way Nahla died," I said.

"I'm not giving up my daily brew," Bertoli said. "Nor my pizza."

"Strong caffeine and carb rich cheese feasts are a heady combination," I said.

Bertoli nodded, seeming happy to lounge and do no work. It was most unlike him.

"Have you noticed anything strange going on around town since Verity's teashop opened?" I read through the leaflet. It was promoting a three-day event featuring all things fungi.

"Crimson Cove isn't your average town," Bertoli said after he'd finished his cookie. "You need to be more specific. What particular brand of strange are you thinking about?"

"At animal control, we've had way more jobs coming in. Animals behaving irrationally and, sometimes, their bonded magic users, too.

Everyone seems tense and not behaving like themselves."

"It could be a moon phase," Bertoli said. "You see it with the werewolves. They can get testy. You sure you don't want a cookie?"

"Are there any meat-flavored cookies?" Sage asked.

"That would be gross," Bertoli said.

"No cookies for us," I said. "We're on a mission."

"You're missing out. They're excellent."

"I'm sure they are. Getting back to the investigation, we've got two murders to deal with, but I see a bigger pattern emerging. Things we shouldn't overlook. It's all connected."

"I don't see any patterns," Bertoli said.

"There's more work than we can handle at animal control. Cythera has been complaining for weeks that you're busier than normal, especially at night, with locals stirring problems."

"That's high spirits," Bertoli said. "And if this strange behavior is because of a moon phase, it'll soon be over."

"A moon cycle doesn't last for weeks," I said. "What if this is all interlinked?"

Bertoli's gaze went to the kitchen. "What is connected to what? I don't get it."

I huffed out a breath. "I don't know! But trouble is building."

"It started at the pizza parlor," Sage said. "The food getting contaminated and no-one taking the blame."

I nodded. "We never got to the bottom of why an ancient vampire was almost vanquished because the wrong herbs got onto the wrong pizzas."

"Nothing started anywhere. That pizza business was explained away," Bertoli said.

"Was it?"

He stood. "The case is closed. Besides, Altruist wasn't murdered. It was a misunderstanding. Are you sure you don't want any cookies?"

"Stop thinking about your belly!"

Bertoli scowled at me. "Why are you obsessing over an old case?"

"It wasn't solved to my satisfaction. We put the mess down to a misunderstanding. What if it wasn't? And now we have other strange behavior going on."

"No we don't."

"Look around you. Where are all your colleagues?" I asked. "And if you visit Vorana's house, all Vorana, Sorcha, and Zandra are talking about is leaving. They want to quit their jobs, sell their businesses, and move away."

"Oh! You're having trouble at home," Bertoli said. "I'm sorry to hear that. I can see how that would be unsettling. A cookie will make you feel better."

"I'll shove those cookies where the sun doesn't shine if you offer them to us again," Sage said. "I'm starving, and a gross, sugar-sweetened breakfast cookie won't fill the gnawing hole in my stomach."

Bertoli shrugged. "You both need to relax. You're so tense."

"I'm rarely tense. You're normally tenser than all of us." I cocked my head. "Although, not recently. You've been shockingly pleasant to work with.

And here you are, kicking back and relaxing when there's a double murder to solve. You're more interested in cookies and this mushroom festival than figuring out who the killer is."

"I've learned that life is too short," Bertoli said. "And we've got the killers in custody. We just need them to crack and confess. Then we can look forward to this fungi festival. It's being promoted everywhere. It'll bring in a huge crowd."

"This is a waste of time," Sage muttered into my ear. "All this dude is interested in is food and partying with mushrooms."

I had to agree. I'd never seen this side of Bertoli before. Was he being affected by whatever was creeping through Crimson Cove, too?

"I'm getting a... something from the kitchen." Bertoli strode away, and we slipped out of the door and left Angel Force.

"Can I go to sleep now?" Sage asked.

"If you wish to return to your dank pile of old newspapers and sulk in a corner, being miserable, be my guest," I said.

"That shed is homey. I could be comfortable out there with the right furnishing. At least until Vorana comes to her senses."

I grunted. "I may join you. Zandra suggested we move in together when she leaves Crimson Cove. I fear she plans to leave me behind when she goes."

"I should warn you, I like my own space. And I get gassy when I eat tinned pilchards." Sage trundled away, her head down. "And the corner I've picked is mine, so keep your paws off."

I turned in the other direction and spotted Griffin hurrying along with several folders and papers in his hands. He missed his step off the curb and tripped, sending the papers flying.

I trotted over to assist him, even though my paws would be of little use. "Those high curbs sometimes trick me as well."

Griffin jumped. "Oh! It's you. That was my fault. I wasn't looking where I was going."

"I expect you have a lot on your mind." I stood on a piece of paper to prevent it from blowing away. It was a letter inviting Griffin to a final interview for the role of personal assistant to a CEO.

He eased it out from under my paw. "Thanks, but I've got it."

"I thought you were happy working with Nahla?" I watched him tuck the letter away.

Griffin held the papers close to his chest. "I was. I'm... I'm looking for a new position now she's dead. I can't afford to be out of work for too long. And I like to keep busy."

I looked at the papers. "That letter said final interview, which suggests you've been to previous interviews. Surely, they can't all have been held within the last few days."

Griffin turned and hurried away. "Maybe they have. That's none of your business."

I pursued him. "Verity and Ivan are in custody for a double murder."

He stopped and looked at me. "Two murders? Who else is dead?"

"Petra was found murdered last night."

His mouth dropped open. "I had no clue. What happened to her?"

"We're not sure. Something deeply unpleasant, though. Definitely not an accident."

"And you think Verity and Ivan were involved?"

"It's possible. Did you know about their affair?"

His eyes widened. "Ivan would never cheat on Nahla. He followed her everywhere."

"He cheated. Ivan and Verity are tangled in something unpleasant." I stared at the papers again. "But if you were miserable working with Nahla, maybe you have a better motive for murdering her."

His nervous composure shattered, and he staggered back and hit a wall. "It wasn't me!"

I stepped closer. "Do you think it was Verity?"

"I... I don't know."

"Ivan?"

"No! Maybe. I... I'm not involved in any of this." Griffin drew in a shaky breath. "I can't believe it was them, though. Do you have proof?"

"We're getting there. They got caught out in a huge lie. And if they've been carrying on behind Nahla's back for a long time..." I let him fill in the blanks.

Griffin gulped. "Nahla would have hated that. If Ivan cheated, it would have shattered her perfect world. She... she wasn't always easy to love."

"Talk to me. Ever since I met you, you've lived on your nerves. That's no way to be. Why are you so nervous all the time?"

Griffin slid slowly down the wall until he was crouched, his head down. "I'm glad Nahla is dead. And I'm glad someone killed her. She deserved it.

And I hope it hurt." With that damning comment, he burst into tears.

Chapter 18

Unveiling the lies

Having such a sturdy, emotionally uptight witch as my forever companion, I rarely saw tears, but I let Griffin weep for several minutes until he got himself under control, allowing him to stroke my silky fur to comfort his fragile emotions.

"You have a lot to get off your chest," I said. "It sounds like Nahla wasn't quite the delight to work for that you told us she was."

Griffin sniffed back tears and loudly blew his nose. "I feel like I'm going to explode. I admitted defeat a long time ago, accepting my fate and making the best of it, but now Nahla is dead. I have a chance. I can finally be free."

More tears ensued, and I was unable to get any sense out of him for several more minutes.

"In times of crisis, my witch turns to comfort food. Would you like some? A big stodgy cake or a slice of pie? You may feel better after you've eaten."

He gulped back his feelings. "I am hungry. I barely had any dinner last night."

"I know just the place to go for the perfect iced cinnamon roll and a large mug of coffee. How does that sound? Get you fueled up and then we can figure out exactly what's going on."

Griffin blinked his watery eyes and nodded, content to follow me along the road to Tia and Binky's bakery. It was early, but Tia opened with the sun. She did most of the baking on-site and always had an eager crowd waiting for her perfectly warm pastries to start their day.

I placed an order with Tia, noting there was no sign of Binky. In a way, I was glad. Our last interaction hadn't been positive. That was something else on my list of things to do. Figure out why my friends were being so shady.

Once we were settled at a small table tucked at the back of the bakery where we wouldn't be disturbed, Griffin demolished half of the giant iced cinnamon roll, and I let the sugar and caffeine kick in before delving into my questions.

"Tell me what you really thought about Nahla," I asked. "And don't worry, I'm not official law enforcement, so I can't arrest you or use your words against you."

"You're not bonded to an angel?"

"Angels don't bond with familiars. I'm with a witch. A wonderful witch who has a lot on her mind, too. Let me help," I said. "Something strange is going on in this investigation, and we must get to the bottom of it. Especially now someone else has died."

Griffin took a few seconds to drink his coffee. His hand was shaking as he lowered the mug to the table. "Nahla was awful. And so controlling. At first, when I started working for her, I was glad she was so hands-on. I had some experience, but it was a shock to be exposed to her world. She was soaring to the top, and I was clinging on and hoping to keep up and not make too many mistakes."

"But she became overbearing?"

"It never stopped. Nahla controlled everyone and everything around her. No one was safe. It had to be her way, or you were gone. And she refused to negotiate about anything. She was ruthless."

"Why didn't you leave your job?" I asked. "It sounds like a miserable existence."

"I tried! So many times. I became frustrated by her iron grip on me, but I thought it would look strange on my resume to leave a job when I'd only been there a short amount of time, so I stuck it out for a year before looking around. I got accepted to an interview, and they offered me the position."

"But you stayed with Nahla?"

"She forced me to stay. I put her down as a referee for my new employer, but she refused to give me a reference and said I didn't deserve one. I was stunned." Griffin shook his head. "Nahla said I should be flattered she was going to such an effort to keep me. She even gave me a small pay raise and said I was valued and to forget about leaving. I was part of the family, and she'd never let me go."

"That's creepy."

"Right! But back then, it got me wondering if I was being paranoid and touchy. Was that just how stars' worlds worked? They were successful because they controlled everything and left nothing to chance."

"Things didn't get better even though you stayed?"

"No. I managed another two years, but Nahla was the same as always. Maybe even worse. I went for another job and got the same result. This time, Nahla was angry when I requested a reference. She called me ungrateful and said other people longed to be in my position, and didn't I know how lucky I was?"

"How did you respond?" I asked.

"I told her to let me go and give the job to one of them. We were a bad fit. It didn't work, and she refused to help me. But I kept trying for another couple of years." Griffin's eyes filled with tears. "I found what looked like an amazing job. I got on well with the interviewer, and he liked me so much that he offered me the job at the end of the interview. I was shaking with excitement as I walked away. I knew things had to change."

"What did you do?" I leaned closer, intrigued by Griffin's story.

"I resigned! I handed Nahla my letter of resignation and told her I was going. I said I'd worked hard for her, and I deserved an excellent reference. I'd done everything she asked me, never complained about working overtime and not getting paid, and I never argued back. But I was done being trodden on, and I wanted out."

"Since you're still here, it's safe to assume that tactic failed."

"Nahla went quiet, and that's always scary. Then she said she'd write me a reference. I was so shocked, I could only blurt out a thank you and give her the details of my new place of work." Griffin lowered his head. "The next morning, I got a message. The position was no longer available. I was thanked for my time, and that was it. I was so surprised that I rang the company and insisted I speak to the man who interviewed me."

"Nahla's reference wasn't glowing?" I asked.

"At first, the interviewer wouldn't talk to me, so I went to the office during my lunch break and confronted him. It was probably the most awkward conversation I've ever had. He tried to brush me off, but then he relented. He showed me the reference Nahla supplied. He said he was so upset by the content and couldn't believe the man he'd interviewed was the same person."

"Nahla ruined your chance," I said, "and trapped you in a job you despise."

"The reference meant the company would never hire me. She said I was lazy, rude, my work was substandard, and I was a thief! There was no way out." Griffin drew in a wobbly breath. "After that, I gave up. I've been with her for almost twenty horrible, tense, scary years. And it's not just me. She trapped everyone. Once Nahla had you in her clutches, she never let you go."

"Nahla seemed so pleasant when I met her," I said. "It was all a front?"

Several tears slid down Griffin's cheeks. "If you walked away, she'd see to it that you left with nothing. She even held back pay as revenge for anyone who had the courage to go. She never gave anyone a reference. Not a good one, anyway. I imagine the people who got out struggled. Nahla had influence in the magic community. She'd spread word that they weren't to be trusted or hired."

"But you applied for another position recently. Why bother if you knew what the outcome would be?"

"Nahla had been particularly cruel, and I snapped. I'd seen the job and thought it looked great, but I didn't apply. After she'd torn me to shreds over something stupid, I stamped off and sent in an application." He shrugged again. "Call it an act of defiance, but I needed to see if I had any control over my life and if anyone considered me worthy."

While Griffin finished his cinnamon bun, I considered this information. It gave him an excellent motive for killing Nahla, but what about Petra? Why would he have wanted her dead?

"Did you have any issues with Petra?" I asked.

"I never had much to do with her. Why do you ask?"

"I mentioned that Petra was murdered, too. I'm looking for who killed her."

Griffin almost dropped his mug before lowering it with both hands to the table. "You can't think it was me."

"I've yet to find your motive. Do you have one?"

"No! I'm not a killer. I'm too timid for that."

I wasn't sure I believed him. You always had to watch the quiet ones. They saw everything and missed nothing.

"What happened to Petra?" Griffin asked.

"Angel Force is investigating. Whoever killed her was ruthless."

He stared over my head, his body shaking. "If Nahla was still alive, I'd instantly think she'd done it. She'd go to any lengths to get her way. And Petra was an irritation. She was one person Nahla couldn't control. Petra was just as feisty as Nahla. She had her own ambitions, and she didn't want anyone stopping her."

"Someone stopped her," I said. "Although if they were both alive, they'd have needed to come to a truce, since Amy recently took on Petra as a client to fill the gaps as Nahla moved toward retirement."

"That's another one who stood her ground with Nahla," Griffin said. "Amy has been in the business for decades, so she knows how to handle difficult types. They'd recently been locking horns because of Nahla's plan to semi-retire. Amy hated that prospect."

I flicked my tail. "That's not what she told me."

"Amy always keeps things professional." Griffin glanced around, but we were the only two sitting at any of the tables. "And rumor has it, Nahla was planning on firing Amy and getting someone easier to manipulate. Even though Amy did all the hard work to make Nahla a household name, she was frustrated because she couldn't control Amy."

"That's interesting," I said. "When Amy was interviewed, she said they had a solid relationship, and she supported Nahla's plans to step back and take things easy."

Griffin's laugh was mirthless. "You could describe both of them as solid. When they clashed, it was like two brick walls slamming into each other. Neither would give ground. And they were always arguing. They put on a front in public, and sometimes, Nahla would grit her teeth and get on with things when Amy secured her a big enough pay check, but they loathed each other."

"Nahla really wasn't popular, was she?"

"If you did everything she told you to do and acted in the way she wanted, you'd be best buddies. But the second you slipped, made a mistake, or did something she wasn't amused by, you got the cold shoulder." Griffin dabbed his eyes with a paper napkin. "It was exhausting working for her. I understood why Amy was moving away from the situation. Nahla wouldn't have been worth the hassle if she planned on working fewer hours."

"What direction was Amy moving in?" I asked.

"A few weeks back, and this is a rumor—the fortunate thing about being a mousy assistant is I'm rarely noticed when people have private conversations—anyway, the rumor is, Amy has signed Petra for a huge deal that Nahla turned down. Nahla was being replaced, and she didn't even know it."

"I've heard similar from someone else," I said. "Would that have bothered Nahla? Since Petra and Nahla were business rivals, she wouldn't want her star to fade too fast."

"I've given that some thought, and I don't think Nahla would have been concerned. She'd made her fortune and gotten her dream life. Whenever anyone talks about famous tea leaf readers, she'll be mentioned. Even if she'd hung up her cup and never read another set of tea leaves, she's created a legacy. It was time to enjoy the spoils with her family."

"I'm glad you're telling me this," I said, "but you must realize it gives you an excellent motive for wanting Nahla dead."

Griffin let out a labored sigh. "I'm glad to unburden. I feel much better. And I know what you're saying. If I didn't have such an airtight alibi, I'd have kept this to myself. But there was no way I could have been involved in that meeting and killing Nahla. I was the meeting coordinator, so I had to be active. There was no time to step out to slay."

"I know Angel Force has checked where you were when Nahla died," I said, "but what about Petra? Her murder happened last night."

"I have no reason to want Petra dead," Griffin said with wide-eyed astonishment. "But I've basically got the same alibi. These events take months of planning and frequent global conferences. I can give you the list of names again, but it was the same people. I wanted Nahla gone from my life but not Petra. She was scary, but she ignored me. That worked for me."

"I'll let the angels know, but they may have a few more questions," I said.

"And I'm happy to answer them." Griffin lifted his coffee mug then realized it was empty, so set it back down. "I'm glad this is almost over, and we can all move on with our lives. I may even be able to get another job now Nahla's not blocking me. I should be sorry she's dead, but she was a monster."

"I understand why you feel that way." I stood and stretched. "And I'm sorry you had to go through all of that with her."

Griffin took out his wallet, but I waved away the offer of reimbursement. The bill had gone on Zandra's tab.

Griffin slid his wallet back inside his jacket pocket. "Before you go, do the angels really think Verity and Ivan killed Nahla?"

"Angel Force is questioning them after some new information has come to light."

"The affair." Griffin shook his head. "I missed that. I can't see Ivan doing it, but given everything Verity went through with Nahla, I'm surprised she didn't do something like this sooner."

"What do you mean? I thought they were friends."

"Oh! No. Well, they made a show of being civil with each other in public, even after the rancid scone review drama."

"That would be enough to taint most friendships," I said. "But there's more to their disharmony?"

Griffin's brow furrowed. "Much more. Verity and Nahla were once related by marriage. You don't know what happened to Verity's brother?"

Chapter 19

Family ties

With shocking new knowledge on board, I almost tripped over my paws in my haste to return to Angel Force. Cythera may not be aware Verity's brother, Daniel, and Nahla had once been married, and the marriage ended in tragedy.

Even though this information damned Verity, there was a niggle in my head that refused to be quiet. But I couldn't ignore this.

I rushed into Angel Force to find the place almost empty. Although it was lunchtime, so most of the angels would be off deciding what to eat, focused on their bellies rather than solving crimes. Fortunately, Cythera was at her desk, staring into space.

"Greetings! I come bearing urgent news," I said.

"Your news is always urgent. What is it this time? You can't decide whether to have the salmon or the chicken for lunch?" Cythera asked.

"I'd always choose the salmon. It's not that." I hopped onto her desk and knocked over a pile of neatly stacked folders.

Cythera glanced at them but didn't scold me or tidy them.

"I've just had an illuminating conversation with Griffin. He hated Nahla and wanted to leave his job," I said. "Once he revealed that secret to me, everything else tumbled out."

"Everything? Do we now know the origins of the universe?"

"Given your lofty status, you'd know how to solve that mystery better than me." I jabbed a clawed paw against her hand. "You don't seem interested in solving these murders."

"That's my job, isn't it? Tell me what genius facts you've unearthed to make yourself even smugger than you already are."

I was too tense to be annoyed by her unpleasant comment. "At first, when I learned Griffin hated Nahla and wanted out of his job, I thought he could be our prime suspect. But you confirmed his alibi for Nahla, and apparently, he was talking to the same people when Petra was murdered. Double-check that alibi, though."

"Yes, sir."

"It's ma'am. But that's not what got me so excited. Did you know Verity had a brother?"

"I don't recall her mentioning him. Why is he important?" Cythera asked.

"Verity's brother, Daniel, used to be married to Nahla."

"And how is that relevant to this investigation?"

"Because he's dead! And Verity blamed Nahla. How's that for a motive?"

"You're making this up. Nahla was married to Ivan."

"Daniel was her first husband. They met when they were young and Nahla was just getting established as a fortune teller. According to Griffin, it was a whirlwind romance, and they married six months after meeting."

Cythera plucked at a loose wing feather. "Why does Verity think Nahla killed her brother?"

"Griffin was unsure how Daniel died, but it was a big scandal, with lots of rumors flying around about the death not being from natural causes. There must be a record of Daniel's death. Griffin said there was an investigation, and Angel Force was all over it because Verity thought something suspicious had gone on," I said. "Daniel wasn't happy being with Nahla and tried to end the marriage. She begged for another chance, so he stuck around for a few more months and then tried to ease himself away. Before he could file for divorce, he died."

Cythera finally stirred to life and stood from her seat. "Give me a few minutes to see if what you're saying is true. If it wasn't a local case, I'll need to get the information sent over."

I followed her as she left the office and filed the request with another angel, who was at his desk, munching on a sandwich.

"This new information, if it's accurate, doesn't change the current situation," Cythera said. "If Verity hated Nahla for what she did to Daniel, then she's guilty. And since I have Verity in a cell, there's no need for any urgency. It's not as if she can run."

"Maybe not." I couldn't disagree with how bad this looked for Verity but still felt dissatisfied.

"Bring me the file when it arrives," Cythera said to the angel.

"Has Verity confessed yet?" I found myself trotting after Cythera like I was a dog, so I deliberately slowed and flicked my tail.

"Not yet. But with this information, it's only a matter of time. Everything is mounting up against her. She'd been foolish not to attempt a plea bargain."

"What about Ivan?" I asked as we went back into her office.

"He's useless. And I'm concerned there's something medically wrong with him. He keeps tripping over his feet, and he's so spaced out. I watched him earlier, and he couldn't even walk a straight line. I sent him to the hospital for tests. When I offloaded him, the doctor seemed concerned. He said there was something wrong with his eyes, so they kept him."

"I wondered the same thing about Ivan," I said. "This rules him out. The way Petra was murdered, it was exacting. It would have needed a precise touch."

"Ivan is the opposite of precise. These murders land squarely on Verity's shoulders." Cythera dropped back into her chair with a sigh. "It would be a tidy end to the case if she turns out to be the killer, especially now we have an even clearer motive for her wanting Nahla out of the way. Not only did Verity want Ivan, she wanted revenge for Nahla killing her brother."

"And that's all thanks to me," I said.

"Quit the smugness. We'd have unearthed that information eventually," Cythera said.

"What about Verity's motive for killing Petra, though?"

Cythera considered the question. "Petra could have attempted a clumsy blackmail attempt, not realizing how dangerous Verity was."

"I suggested the same thing to Sage." I sat back on my haunches. "Verity should be in the movies, because she had me fooled with her nice act. Although she didn't fool Sorcha. She didn't like her. I thought it was professional rivalry, but Sorcha must have seen through the façade."

Cythera gazed out of her office door. "I guess so."

I cocked my head. "You're not excited by this news. This is a breakthrough in the case!"

"This isn't my only case. And I'm stopping for lunch soon. I would have left already if you hadn't bothered me."

I hissed softly at her. "Bothered you? I just helped you solve a double murder."

"My gratitude is unwavering."

"Knock, knock." Roland Moldsworth and Nimbus appeared in the doorway. "I hope I'm not interrupting. You both look serious."

"Fluffy was just leaving," Cythera said.

Roland gave a brief, nervy smile as he held out a pile of papers. "These are the final forms for the mushroom festival. I had to make alterations to the license. I hope it won't be a problem."

"It shouldn't be. You've paid the fees, and so long as you're not planning on selling live animals or dangerous explosives, you're good to go," Cythera said.

Roland gave a panicky chuckle. "Nothing like that. Just fungi. Lots and lots of beautiful fungi. We've had a few last-minute stallholders get involved, though. I wanted to make sure everybody was covered." He smiled at me. "Will you be attending the festival with Zandra?"

I nodded. "She's mentioned wanting to go."

"It's so exciting. Isn't it, Nimbus?"

Nimbus rippled as she growled but made no comment as to her thoughts about the upcoming event.

"I can't stop. Who knew volunteering to arrange a festival would become a full-time job?" Roland left the papers on Cythera's desk and scurried away.

"Everyone seems so into their mushrooms," I murmured.

"It'll be good to have something to look forward to after this murder business is put to bed," Cythera said.

"Until the next one."

There was another knock on the door, and Maverick appeared, beaming a perfectly beautiful smile, his blond lion's mane of hair fluffed around his head. "My darling wife. I've been thinking about you all morning. I bring gifts. Chocolate fudge cupcakes, and look at this. A delightful talking cupcake, too." He held out a soft toy for Cythera.

"Where did you get that?" Cythera didn't take the cupcake.

Maverick dashed over and kissed her cheek. "A gremlin was giving them out. He said he had to clear his former boss's room, so he didn't have to take her things with him when he left town."

"I recognize that cupcake," I said. "That's Nahla's merchandise. She was handing them out at Vorana's bookstore. They talk, don't they?"

Maverick chuckled. "That's my special surprise for my beloved. You can make the cupcake say anything you like." He pressed the middle of the cupcake.

"Every day, in every way, I love you more and more. I love you to the moon and back, around Uranus, and up your Pluto. Wherever you go, I will follow you." The cupcake sing-songed the message before ending with a giggle.

Maverick pressed it again.

"Can you make that thing stop?" Cythera muttered to me.

"Maverick's cupcake is cute. You need to treasure your husband and your talking cupcake," I whispered.

Maverick's brilliant blue eyes sparkled with joy as he set the cupcake on Cythera's desk. "Isn't it adorable?"

Cythera gave the smiling cupcake the evil eye. "It's something. Don't you have jobs back at the house?"

"I've breezed through them. I've also made a plan for dinner. I have a short meeting later this afternoon, but then I'm all yours." He grabbed the soft toy and squeezed it again.

Cythera snatched it away and threw it at me. I caught it mid-air and was almost overcome with the temptation to make biscuits against its softness. It was a high-quality fluffy cupcake.

"Off you go," Cythera said to Maverick. "We're in the middle of an important murder investigation, so I can't afford to be distracted."

"I thought you were about to have lunch," I said.

"I could take you to lunch," Maverick said. "I'm in the mood for pizza. Juno, would you like to join us?"

"Juno misheard. There's no time for lunch. I'll see you later at home." Cythera kept ushering Maverick away and then stomped back to the office. "That was all your fault."

"I'm happy your perfect husband is all my fault, but I'm not entirely sure why you think that."

"You give him dumb ideas. I expect you gave him that ridiculous cupcake just to embarrass me." She picked up the cupcake and threw it against the wall.

"You'll hurt its feelings," I said. "And I haven't seen Maverick for days. I've been too busy trying to solve your murders."

"Since you're so obsessed with these wretched murders, let's see what Verity has to say about Nahla's relationship with Daniel. Has she concealed anything from us?"

"I'm thrilled you're finally accepting there's an us." I dashed away as the cupcake was hurled at me. "I'll be in the kitchen. Yell when you're ready for me." At last, we were back on the case.

After snooping about for treats, I waited a few moments until Cythera had settled Verity into an interview room and then joined them.

Verity had aged ten years overnight. She looked broken. Her hair was limp, and there were bags under her eyes. Was it the guilt making her feel and look so bad?

"We'll keep this short," Cythera said as she sat opposite Verity. I used the table as my seat. "New information has come to light that proves you're guilty of killing Nahla."

"What information?" Verity asked after a few seconds of stunned silence.

"I learned from a reliable source that your brother Daniel and Nahla used to be married," I said.

She paled and swallowed several times. "That's true."

"I've also been informed Daniel was unhappy with Nahla, but she didn't want to let him go. Before he freed himself from the relationship, he died."

"And you wanted that death investigated," Cythera said. "I requested the file on the case and have looked through it. You made numerous complaints about how Angel Force mishandled the investigation. Even though your brother's death was ruled an accident, you remained unhappy."

Verity looked down at the table. "I was broken up about what happened to Daniel for a long time, but I forgave Nahla."

"Why did you think she was involved in what happened to Daniel?" I'd have liked to have seen the file, but Cythera had inconsiderately left me out.

"It was her tea," Verity said. "Nahla was such a powerful fortune teller. She used rare and expensive blends of tea with her clients. She charged so much because of the quality of the product she used. I had no problem with her wanting to do the best for her clients, but the tea's purity made it potent. And if you weren't used to it and didn't take the proper precautions, it could be deadly."

"Go on," I said.

"Nahla didn't know how fragile Daniel was," Verity said, the sad tone in her voice hurting my heart. "When he was a teenager, Daniel fell in with the wrong crowd and used illegal substances. He got hooked. It took us years to get him clean. And you know how the saying goes."

"Once an addict, always an addict," I murmured.

Verity nodded. "He was doing well, but then he met Nahla, and she introduced him to her tea blends. Those blends are very drinkable. She didn't just use them to tell fortunes, especially not when starting out. She'd also whip up a blend if someone was struggling. Maybe it was stress because they had an interview or an important test. She'd find the right combination of herbs and magic, and they'd buy it from her."

"I'm not sure that's legal," Cythera said.

"It is. Nahla never used anything she shouldn't in her teas. And for most people, that wouldn't have been a problem," Verity said.

"But Daniel became intoxicated by her tea blends?" I asked.

"He wouldn't stop drinking her enchanted blends," Verity said. "I told him to be careful, but he laughed it off. He said it was tea, and nothing bad would happen to him. I even asked Nahla to be more careful and to keep her teas away from him. She also didn't see the problem."

"What went wrong?" I asked.

"I'll never know for certain, but things hadn't been good between them for a few months. Daniel spoke to me about moving in to get some space and figure out if he even wanted to be married to her." Verity wiped away a tear. "I welcomed him in. I said he could have a spare room for as long as he needed. But I refused to let him bring the enchanted tea."

"What did it do to him?" I asked.

"He'd walk around daydreaming most of the time, coming up with these fantasies and ridiculous ideas. He barely stepped foot into reality. He lost his job, and most of his friends abandoned him until all he had left were a few family members and Nahla."

"In the file, there was a statement from you that claims Nahla used a potent blend of tea to kill Daniel," Cythera said. "Do you still believe that?"

Verity heaved out a sigh. "I was angry when I said that. But I'd seen Daniel the day before he died, and he had this enormous pot of tea he kept refilling. He said it was delicious. It made him feel calm, happy, and as if he didn't have a care in the world. I'd asked him to stop so many times, so I didn't say anything. It's no use forcing a person to get help if they're not ready. Instead, I told him to be careful and that I loved him, and then I left. I got a call early the next morning to say he'd died in his sleep."

Cythera flicked through the file she'd brought in with her. "Massive amounts of various types of tea blends were found in his system. None of it was ruled toxic or dangerous, though."

"I didn't believe that at the time," Verity said. "I was furious. At Nahla. Daniel. But most of all, myself. If I'd said something that day, begged him one more time to stop using so much enchanted tea, he'd still be here. But I didn't. I let him down."

"You didn't let him down," I said. "And you're right. Unless a person is ready to accept help and change, all your efforts will fail. Daniel got caught in another cycle of addiction, and he wasn't ready to break free."

Verity dabbed away more tears. "I was furious with Nahla for a long time, but I saw the reports, and I spoke to the angels who investigated, and I finally realized no one was to blame. It was a tragic accident."

Cythera slapped the file shut and shook her head. "You're lying. And you're guilty of murder. Confess to both murders and make this easy on yourself. Given the circumstances around your brother's death, a judge may feel sorry for you."

Verity jerked back in her seat as if she'd been slapped. "I didn't kill anyone. You'll never get a confession out of me."

"I doubt we'll even need one," Cythera said. "Thanks to the fluffy here and the evidence we've gathered, you're going away, and you're never getting out. Say goodbye to your freedom. Good riddance."

A sob choked out of Verity as an angel came in and took her back to her cell.

"That was harsh," I said.

"You can go, too," Cythera said. "It's just paperwork and processing to complete. You'll reap the glory as always, and I'll do the real work."

I watched Cythera stomp out of the room. This was a conclusion of sorts, but it didn't feel victorious. We had the pieces to this mystery in our paws, but somehow, although we'd forced them to fit together, something felt off about this whole investigation. Including Cythera's lousy attitude.

Chapter 20

Soft surprise

"This is the perfect spot for a date. I'm glad you brought me up here." I leaned against Sammy as we sat snuggled on the bakery rooftop, looking out across Crimson Cove. The sun was just setting, bathing the town in an intense robe of orange.

"You seemed distressed when you told me about what's been going on in the investigation," Sammy said. "And it must have been a shock to find Petra on the beach. I figured you deserved a treat."

I nodded. An enchanted cat was never happier than when she was up high, observing her domain and putting the world to rights with her favorite fluffy companion.

"These murders have me stumped," I said. "Cythera is convinced Verity is the mastermind behind it. And the evidence points to her, as do some of the other suspects. Should I accept Verity is our killer and let the angels finish things?"

"If your instincts tell you otherwise, you shouldn't ignore them," Sammy said. "That's one thing cats excel at. We sense when something is off. It's saved my skin plenty of times."

I gently sighed. Not being born a cat had its disadvantages. "We've gotten things muddled. I don't know how, and I don't know what parts I've gotten wrong, but Verity seemed so distraught when we interviewed her. She's normally such a joyful person, but she seemed defeated."

"It's damning her brother died in his sleep because of Nahla's herbal tea. Verity may say she forgave Nahla, but it must be tough to move past that. I doubt I could."

"Many people would find it impossible," I said. "I fear Cythera will have charged Verity by the end of today even without a confession."

"What about her accomplice, Ivan?"

"He's at the hospital, being medically assessed. I'd like to speak to him again, but from all accounts, he's useless. If he can't even walk straight, he can't effectively kill."

"It could be shock making him behave like that," Sammy said. "It does weird things to people. I remember when I was smaller and timid, I'd shake all day after I'd done something stressful. Then the next day, I'd sleep for hours. It was my body's way of forcing me to decompress."

The bakery door slammed open, and Binky and Archie bounded out, roughly play fighting. They charged a group of unsuspecting passersby, causing them to scream and scatter. Archie grabbed one unfortunate fellow and shook him roughly by his collar.

I stood and watched the scene, frowning. "What's gotten into them? Archie can be clumsy, but he's never deliberately cruel."

Sammy sighed. "It's not just them. I know you've been preoccupied with this case, but lots of people are acting strangely. I've been keeping out of the way, focusing on my community service, and ensuring my nose stays clean, though. I can't afford to get in trouble again."

"That's sensible." I glared at Archie and Binky as they bounded along the street, crashing into each other. Binky slammed against a store window, and I winced, thinking it had cracked, but it survived the enormous impact. "Perhaps their behavior is a lingering aftereffect of those strange truffles on the pizzas. Archie ate an enormous amount of the special pizza Voss made for Remus and his vampire visitors."

"That must be out of his system by now," Sammy said.

I glanced at Sammy. "Did you eat any of that odd pizza when it was doing the rounds?"

He shook his head. "Don't you remember? I was ordered home, so I couldn't help. I had to be in before curfew."

"Of course. You can't risk breaking curfew so close to the end of your service." I gazed along the street. Archie had tipped over a large trash container, and Binky was shooting random blasts of magic in the air. "When we have a moment, we must investigate what's going on with those two."

"You need to solve these murders first," Sammy said.

"I will. I've yet to meet a case that's defeated me." Although this one felt like it was about to. It was slipping through my paws, and I was undecided whether to let it go or try once more to get to the bottom of what was going on.

"The sun's setting. I need to get home," Sammy said. "Will you be okay?"

"I'm much better having spent time with you. Thank you again." I glanced back at the empty treat bowl Sammy had generously provided for our date. He was a sweet cat, and I was fortunate to have him in my life.

After exchanging a fond farewell, I trotted to the small hospital set on the edge of Crimson Cove. It was time to visit the patient. I wanted to know Ivan's thoughts about Verity. Perhaps he'd heard her sneaking out on the night they were together, creeping to the beach to confront and kill Petra. If he could confirm Verity had left him alone that night, then I had no option but to believe she was behind all of this.

The hospital didn't welcome four-legged visitors, so I used a little stealth and magic to get past the nurse at the desk. It was minimally staffed, since minor ailments could be easily fixed with magical herbs or spells, but serious medical issues were always brought here, especially when tainted with magic.

It took me a few minutes of searching before I came to a door heavily enchanted to prevent access.

"You can't go in there."

I turned and discovered an elderly male doctor ambling toward me. "I'm looking for a patient. Ivan Gerbolt."

"That's my patient. You're connected to Ivan? Are you his familiar?"

"Temporary helpful assistant," I said. "I was told by Angel Force he'd been brought in for a medical assessment. I was wondering how he was doing."

"Not good. And he's behind that door," the doctor said. "You work for Angel Force?"

"They only hire the best," I said. "What's wrong with him?"

"I shouldn't tell you. Patient confidentiality."

"Cythera will be unhappy to learn the investigation is stuck because I couldn't get the information I needed," I said. "We're deciding whether to charge Ivan with a double murder."

The doctor grimaced. "I've tangled with Cythera one too many times to know about her sour moods. And the last time we spoke, she was downright rude. She's always blunt and straight to the point, but calling someone a crusty old badger who should have retired twenty years ago won't get her the information she needs."

I held in a startled laugh. I couldn't imagine those words ever coming out of Cythera's mouth. "What did you do to upset her?"

"Nothing! She's been pestering me about the information you're after. She wants to know if Ivan is fit to make a statement and if he was capable of murder."

"And what's your expert opinion?" I asked.

He gave a weary sigh. "I need coffee. I've been here since dawn. Two doctors are on vacation at the same time. I'm left to do all the work while they sun themselves in their thongs."

I followed him along the corridor. "I'll get out of your way as soon as I have the information. How bad is Ivan?"

The doctor didn't speak as he went into the kitchen and made himself a cup of coffee before sitting at the table. "He keeps having strange outbursts. We've put him through a barrage of tests, and we've discovered his magic is dangerously unstable."

"That's the reason he seems so dopey?" I asked. "I was there when Angel Force arrested him and Verity. He could barely stand."

"It's so bad, I'm not sure he'll make it."

My eyes widened. "What caused such instability?"

The doctor slurped down his coffee. "If sharing this with you comes back to bite me in the behind, I'll deny everything."

"I assure you, Cythera trusts me with all her secrets," I said. "I was even at her wedding."

"The whole town was at her wedding," he said. "I'm still running through the results, but Ivan has too much magic in his system that doesn't belong to him."

"Is it from the blended tea he drinks?" I asked. "His late wife, Nahla, was a talented tea leaf reader. Ivan enjoyed sampling that tea."

"That's in the mix, but there's other magic there, too."

"What kind of magic are we talking about?"

"From what I've picked out so far, it's a type of control spell. A grossly powerful spell that's been used for a long time."

"It's unlikely he'd use magic of that sort on himself," I said.

"I suspect someone has been dosing him with it," the doctor said. "His problems began as the magic levels shifted. If you get a regular dose of a control spell, you don't notice its effects. But it's addictive magic, so if you miss a few doses, it'll knock you off balance."

"Literally in Ivan's case," I said.

"There's a hefty magical imbalance in him," the doctor said. "And it's gotten so bad, we're having to protect the patients and the staff by locking him up. He's showing signs of being an unstable addict. I'm not sure we can bring him back from this."

"I insist on seeing him," I said. "Ivan's a key witness in an active investigation. I need answers from him."

The doctor checked the time. "My shift ended three minutes ago."

"Does that mean you're off duty? Would you unofficially help a cat out and let me speak to Ivan?"

"If you go in there, I won't be able to protect you," the doctor said. "Ivan yells at the staff and throws out these weird spells. They don't seem effective, but they sting if they hit you. All his magic is warped beyond repair."

"Anything can be fixed with enough time and patience. And I take full responsibility for any injuries sustained, but I really need to speak to Ivan."

The doctor downed his coffee. "What the heck. If you can figure out what's wrong with him and get him out of here, it'll be one less problem for me to tackle."

With a delighted flick of my tail, I followed him back to the locked room. He removed the magic locks, cracked open the door, and pointed inside. "Last door on the right. Be careful."

"Your help is appreciated." I hurried into the corridor, and the door clicked shut behind me. The help was welcome but also strange. This hospital was a stickler for their rules to ensure patients were kept safe. Was this doctor someone else behaving out of character?

I had no time to dwell on that possibility. I needed to get to Ivan and see if he was keeping secrets. I stopped by the door, and my fur bristled. Even though the door was closed, I saw sparks of light flashing intermittently from beneath the gap.

I inched it open and discovered the magic was sparking off Ivan. He lay on a single hospital bed, his eyes open. He was clutching one of Nahla's soft toy cupcakes.

I trotted to the bed and hopped onto it. "Greetings!"

Ivan stared at me, not seeming to comprehend what he was seeing. "Are... are you real?"

"As real as I am glorious. Do you remember me?"

His glassy eyes wouldn't focus. "If you're real, you look like the cat who arrested me."

"I don't have the formidable power to detain, but I was there when the angels brought you in. I heard from the doctor that you're struggling with your magic." I ducked as an orange spark pinged close to me. It stank of rank honey and curry spice.

"No more than usual. My magic has been strange for years. This is the worst it's been for a while, though." Ivan lifted a hand and stared at it as if it was the most bizarre thing he'd ever encountered.

"I'm sorry to hear that." More magic sparked off Ivan and whacked into me. It did sting, and I swiftly brushed it away with a paw.

"Sorry. I've got no control. I don't know what's wrong with me. I feel so strange."

"The doctors think you've been drugged," I said.

"Who would want to drug me?" He squeezed the cupcake.

"Love you forever, honey bun," came Nahla's voice from the toy. It was strange hearing a dead woman's voice drift out of a soft toy.

"I'm figuring that out. I thought you'd like to know Angel Force is on the verge of charging Verity with Nahla and Petra's murders." I hoped a little shock might prompt clarity.

"Oh! That's sad. I like Verity. She's always so nice to me and makes me feel noticed. Most people write me off as Nahla's husband. But I have a name. It's... Ivan. It is Ivan, isn't it?"

"It is. Well done for remembering. Can you also recall if Verity went out on the evening you were together? It would only have needed to be for half an hour."

"My memory's gone. Verity could have vanished for hours and I don't remember. I can't get my thoughts in order." Ivan gently bashed the toy cupcake against his head. "I don't feel right."

"The doctors are looking for a way to fix you," I said. "What about something Verity said? Has she hinted that she wanted Nahla or Petra dead?"

Ivan closed his eyes for a long time. "Nope."

"Has Verity told you about Daniel?"

Ivan cracked open an eye. "Her brother?"

I nodded.

"We talked about it. But she resolved things. She moved on from all of that. Verity is as sweet as this cupcake."

"Did she tell you she'd moved on?"

Ivan considered the question, his magic sparking and fizzling around us, but aimed at nothing. "Verity said it was hard, but she couldn't live in the past and be full of anger. I admired her for that. I don't think I'd have been strong enough." He grimaced as more magic flared out of him. "I feel so sick."

I settled my paws on his legs and covered him with a wave of calming magic to ease the tension in his shoulders. "What about Petra? Did Verity ever say she had issues with her?"

Ivan closed his eyes again and clutched the cupcake. "I don't think so. But I don't even know my own thoughts anymore." A blast of magic flared out of him, so violent that it knocked me onto the floor and dug into my paws until I flicked it away. The magic burned this time. There was power behind it.

A second later, the talking cupcake slammed into me, knocking me over again.

Ivan lurched out of the bed, a snarl on his face. "Hate them all. Everything is wrong. I'm wrong. Why do I feel like this? Help me!"

I stood on the cupcake, and Nahla's disembodied voice repeated the sweet sentence.

"Can you remember when you first started feeling like this?" I asked.

"I've always felt like this!" Ivan whacked the flat of his hand against his forehead. "I can't remember when I didn't feel wrong."

"For as long as you've been married to Nahla? When you were younger? Any clue could help the doctor figure out what's going on."

"At least a decade." He flopped onto the bed, all his anger gone. "I'm going to sleep now. Sort of hoping I won't wake up."

"Pleasant dreams," I murmured as I softly kneaded the cupcake, and Nahla's voice came out again.

I stared at the smiling cupcake and pressed it again, listening intently to the voice. The realization hit me almost as hard as Ivan's spell. I had one thing to check, but if I was right, I'd figured out who our killer was, and I almost agreed with their reason for committing murder.

Chapter 21

Cake confession

"Anyone would think you were in charge of Angel Force, given how bossy you've been lately." Cythera stood outside Ivan's hospital room as we waited for Bertoli to gather the suspects.

"I sometimes feel like I am." I flicked my tail back and forth. "Particularly with this case. And you've let most of your angels vanish from the office, rather than focus on solving this perplexing crime."

Cythera shrugged. "We're all busy. And we didn't have to bring everybody here to solve this. Why not just tell me the facts so I can make an arrest?"

"Where's the joy in that? Besides, I've earned this."

"You always have to show off when you reveal a killer."

"This isn't me showboating. You've seen the state Ivan is in. The doctor had to strap him to the bed and magically sedate him. He's about to break apart, so there was no way he could be moved. This works."

She tapped a white-booted foot on the floor, suggesting she had better things to do than figure out who committed a double murder.

I walked away, uncharacteristically anxious. When I'd fitted the final piece of the puzzle into place, I'd raced home to tell Zandra, but she hadn't been there. Nobody had been home. It felt strange solving a crime without my witch by my side, and an increasingly surly, disinterested Cythera was a poor substitute.

Bertoli strolled along the corridor, accompanied by an anxious-looking Griffin, an irritated Amy, and a worried Verity. Sorcha trailed behind them, dragging her feet.

"What took you so long?" I said to Bertoli.

"We stopped for snacks. I was hungry."

Bertoli rarely let himself get distracted from work and never for food. "You're here now. Take everyone into Ivan's room."

"When we're done here, I'll find a way to get rid of Juno," Cythera whispered all too loudly to Bertoli, ensuring I overheard her rudeness.

I whacked her in the behind with a spell. "Behave yourself. I'm about to solve this crime for you."

Cythera flared her wings at me then strode after the suspects.

I caught Sorcha just before she went in. "Have you seen Zandra?"

She shook her head. "Maybe she's gone for a job interview. She'd called to get details about several positions."

"I hope it's not that," I said. "I still can't figure out why Zandra's so desperate to leave Crimson Cove."

"She's got the right idea," Sorcha said. "I'm rethinking my place here after being involved in this mess. Who wants to remain in a town where people think you're a killer?"

"Perhaps once we have the actual killer behind bars, you'll be less unsettled," I said.

"We'll see. I'm looking at all options. Let's get this over with, shall we?"

I followed Sorcha into the hospital room. Everyone had gathered to the far side of the room, away from Ivan's bed. I understood why. He was writhing like an eel caught on an electric wire as magic sparked out of him. Despite the doctor giving him a heavy magical sedative, he couldn't settle. He was lost in his addiction.

"Get on with it." Cythera gestured at me. "Tell us Verity killed Nahla and Petra and you have the evidence to prove it."

Verity opened her mouth to protest, but I shook my head to stop her. "When Nahla arrived in Crimson Cove, she appeared to have the world at her feet. A thriving career, a supportive team, and a loving husband. All of that was a front. When I scraped the surface, I discovered her life was anything but perfection."

"There's no need for the dramatics," Cythera said. "Hurry up. I've got places to be."

I speared her with a fearsome look. "At first, there were concerns about Sorcha being involved in Nahla's murder. Unfortunately, Angel Force got it into their heads that, because Sorcha had an issue with Verity, she decided to kill Nahla to ruin the upcoming festival and then frame Verity for the murder."

"Which I decided was wrong, so I focused on Verity," Cythera said. "And I was right to do so."

I raised a paw. "Sorcha is innocent. She has reliable witnesses who heard her in the café at the time of Nahla's murder."

"Those witnesses are vampires. I've never trusted vampires," Cythera said.

"You're never one to reveal prejudice," I said. "Don't start now. It's deeply unattractive."

Cythera huffed out a breath but kept her mouth shut.

"I was more interested in Petra as Nahla's killer. Her behavior displayed an intense dislike for Nahla. It would have been easy to pin the blame on her, especially when she disappeared not long after she'd been interviewed by Angel Force."

"It wasn't Petra?" Verity asked.

"The prisoner must remain silent," Cythera said.

"Verity isn't a prisoner," I snapped. "Merely a suspect."

"She's about to be charged with a double murder," Cythera said.

Cythera's truculent behavior made me want to zap her in the behind again. "Petra must have realized she was about to become the prime suspect, so she stayed away, hoping Nahla's killer would be found and she'd be in the clear."

Ivan groaned and writhed on the bed, and I had to dodge a spark of magic that shot out of him to avoid getting my fur singed.

"We were all set, and I include myself in that we, to find Petra and charge her with Nahla's murder. But then we come to the twist. Our prime suspect was also killed."

"Petra could still be guilty," Sorcha said. "She was around at the time of Nahla's murder. And, as you said, they didn't get along."

"But Petra was at your café on the night of Nahla's murder," I said.

"Petra had a tongue as sharp as her mind," Amy said. "I'm surprised it hasn't gotten her into trouble before now."

"We'll get to what happened to Petra in a moment," I said. "Griffin, you lied when you said you were happy working for Nahla. When I discovered you'd been applying for other jobs, you confessed how much you despised working for her and how terribly she treated you. You were stuck working for her because you had no other option. That must have been a horrible experience."

Griffin's hand shook as he dabbed at his sweaty brow. "I knew it would look bad if I revealed what an awful position I was in. But I didn't do it! You've checked my alibi for both murders. Yes, I had a motive for wanting Nahla out of my life, but I couldn't have done that to her."

"No, you didn't. And I'm glad you're free to find something that'll make you happy," I said.

"Can we get to the point?" Cythera asked.

I ignored her rudeness. "Amy also had a suitable motive for wanting Nahla dead."

Amy stopped tapping away on her mobile snow globe and lifted her head. "What would that be?"

"You weren't truthful about how happy you were Nahla was retiring," I said. "You told us you supported her, but you were angry about losing such a moneymaker. Nahla was your star, but she no longer wanted to perform."

"I have other stars that perform just as well," Amy said. "I wasn't heading for the poor house because Nahla lost her spark."

"You also failed to reveal you were talking to Petra about becoming Nahla's replacement. You've recently signed her for a promotion meant for Nahla."

"I didn't reveal it because it's none of your business and not relevant to what's going on here," Amy said. "Petra was a talented tea leaf reader. After a few years, Nahla would have become a faded legacy, and Petra would still be shining. If only some idiot hadn't sliced and diced her on your beach, I'd have made a fortune from our partnership."

I looked at Ivan. His body was pulsing. "Several of the suspects in this investigation pointed us to Verity. I was surprised at first. She's been nothing but generous and sweet since she moved to Crimson Cove and opened her tea shop. But then we discovered Verity's affair with Ivan. An affair that has been going on for some time."

Verity traced her tongue across her bottom lip. "Nahla was only ever interested in her career. Ivan is a good person, and he deserves better. We were both lonely. I'm not proud of the affair, but I would never kill another woman to get her man."

"That's exactly what you did," Cythera said. "Ivan most likely told you he wasn't interested anymore.

Maybe Nahla found out and threatened to divorce him unless he dropped you. He wouldn't have hesitated. He would never leave his life of luxury and privilege to live above a teashop in a tedious town like this."

"There's nothing tedious about our marvelous town," I said.

Cythera scowled and gestured for me to hurry.

"Verity and Ivan both have excellent motives for wanting Nahla dead. They could have fallen in love and needed to get rid of an obstacle to their happiness. Nahla could have become difficult or threatening, so they needed her gone."

"No! Nahla never knew about our affair," Verity said. "I promise, she had no idea we were together. We were always discreet."

"She didn't," Ivan murmured.

I turned to see his eyes were open. Magic still sparked out of him, but he appeared focused.

"I was surprised when I heard about the affair," Amy said. "They must have been super sneaky to get away with this. How long has it been going on?"

"About a year," Verity said. "The first time it happened, we said we'd never do it again. We regretted it, but we kept being drawn back to each other. Neither of us wanted things to change, though, and I didn't want Ivan to leave Nahla and marry me. I was content being an independent woman. Besides, Ivan enjoyed the life he'd built with Nahla."

"That's not true," I said. "Ivan wasn't happy, and he had an excellent reason to be miserable. But he had no idea the trouble he'd get himself into when he carried out a murder."

Chapter 22

Close to home

Verity gasped, and even Amy looked mildly startled after I unveiled Ivan as the killer.

"It wasn't Ivan!" Cythera shook her head. "We've established how sick he is. The man can barely get out of bed. He's not capable of killing anyone."

"Ivan discovered a secret Nahla had been keeping from him," I said. "And that secret was so awful he had to kill her. He saw it as the only way out of the situation. And if it weren't for a talking cupcake, I'd have never figured out how he'd done it."

"Now you've lost me," Cythera said. "Are you saying a talking cupcake committed these murders?"

I drew in a breath to avoid snapping at Cythera. She had her stupid head on today. "Ivan is sick because Nahla was drugging him. She used her powerful tea blends to keep him subservient and by her side."

Everyone looked at Ivan. He winced and magic lanced out of him, causing the group to scatter to avoid being struck.

Cythera looked at Verity. "Did Ivan tell you he had a miserable marriage?"

Verity's brow furrowed. "He never talked about much of substance. He's just fun to be with. Occasionally, when we'd been together for a couple of nights, he'd fall into a quiet mood. I'd ask him what was wrong, and he'd say he was thinking about his future. I thought it was just the guilt coming out. He was a married man, and he was with me. But he said once that he saw a future without Nahla. I didn't press him on what he meant because I didn't want him to think I'd replace Nahla. That was never my ambition."

"They argued a lot," Griffin whispered. "When they thought no one was around, they'd bicker. It was mainly Nahla complaining about things Ivan did. I stayed out of it, but I wondered if there was trouble between them. And I always thought Ivan drank a lot to take the edge off their troubles. It wasn't drink making him so spaced out?"

"Nahla was determined to have the perfect life, even if it meant drugging her husband to an unsafe extent to keep him loyal," I said. "The doctors have run extensive tests on Ivan and discovered dangerous doses of magic in his system. Not just from the tea blends, but from powerful control spells Nahla used on him."

"Huh! I always insisted she needed the perfect family for appearance's sake," Amy said. "She told me I had nothing to worry about and everything was under control. I didn't think she meant literally. She really drugged Ivan? For all the years they were married?"

"Nahla didn't want to derail her reputation by having an unruly husband," I said. "She forced so much magic on Ivan that he's become addicted to it. Without the magic Nahla gave him every day, he's dying."

"The doctors can save him, though?" Verity bit her bottom lip, her anxious gaze on Ivan.

"He'll need to go through a long, slow detox process," I said. "And he won't be fit to stand trial for months."

"How does the talking cupcake come into this?" Sorcha asked.

"When Ivan figured out what Nahla was doing to him, he came up with a plan. He created a fake alibi by recording himself snoring and then left it to play on repeat in the hotel. He must have convinced Nahla to return to the bookstore with him, and he drowned her in the cauldron."

"Those wretched cupcakes are always getting stuck on repeat," Amy said. "They drive me insane. You hear them in the boxes, talking to themselves. It's creepy."

"Creepy, but perfect for what Ivan needed to make his plan work. Hotel guests and staff commented on hearing Ivan's snoring, so he must have made it extra loud to ensure it would be noticed to give himself an alibi for that night," I said.

"You can record anything on the cupcakes," Griffin said. "They're fan favorites since you can customize them."

Cythera stomped over to Ivan's bed. "Did you kill Nahla? Has she been drugging you all this time, so you got your revenge?"

Ivan stammered several nonsense words. "She... she said I was her property. She owned me since she paid for my life. I tried to fight her, but my thoughts would muddle. I couldn't get a clear head for long enough to figure out how to escape her control."

"What changed?" Verity slowly approached the bed, a ward up to avoid being whacked by Ivan's misfiring magic. "How did you work out what was happening to him?"

"Nahla must have made a mistake with the dose," I said. "Just enough that Ivan's confusion lifted."

Griffin cleared his throat. "Nahla was recently unwell for a few days. She said it was burnout from too much work. She went to a restorative spa for a long weekend. Before she left, she gave me some potions and said they were Ivan's health tonics. I had to make sure he drank one every day. She was insistent I watch him drink them."

"You didn't think that was odd?" Cythera asked.

"She asked me to do much odder things over the years, so I didn't give it a second thought."

"Nahla needed to keep Ivan under control while she was recovering," I said. "Didn't Ivan want to drink the tonics?"

Griffin grimaced. "I... I didn't give them to him. I got busy, and it slipped my mind. When I realized my error, I panicked and threw them away. When Nahla asked if he'd taken them, I pretended I'd given them to Ivan. It was just before we came to Crimson Cove. Would that have done this to him?"

"That could have been enough to get Ivan to see the light and plan his escape," I said. "By making that mistake, you set him free. Unfortunately, Ivan didn't run. He planned revenge."

"I'm glad she's gone," Ivan muttered. "I hated being a show pony. Please, make me better and then take me away. I'd be content to spend the rest of my life in a quiet cell with no one bothering me ever again. All Nahla loved about me was my looks. I wasn't even a person to her. I was a commodity. A ridiculously handsome commodity."

Cythera glowered at me, not a word of thanks to be had. "And Petra? Why did you kill her?"

Ivan jerked in the bed, and more magic sliced out of him, shattering a glass of water.

That was something I hadn't fully reconciled. "Seeing how unstable Ivan's magic is, if he wandered out of Verity's house without her noticing and ended up on the beach, he could have mistaken Petra for something scary and attacked her. Or it could have been an accident. His magic has been doing odd things."

"Can you translocate?" Cythera asked Ivan.

He nodded. "I used to be able to without giving it a thought. I'm unsure what would happen if I tried now, though. I could bring this hospital down on our heads by mistake. I have power, but Nahla never let me use it."

Cythera stared at him for a long, tense moment. "That's most likely what happened. You were confused, you wandered off and mistook Petra for someone else. Maybe even Nahla."

"Petra smelled like Nahla," I said. "They used similar tea blends. Maybe the smell confused Ivan, and he thought Nahla had returned to haunt him."

As I said those words, I wasn't convinced, but what other option was there?

"That's good enough." Cythera pointed at the bed. "Bertoli, charge Ivan with murder."

⸙

With a spring in my step, I dashed away from the hospital. This good news would cheer up Zandra. I'd convince her Crimson Cove was a safe and happy place to be, and she'd forget all the nonsense about moving and finding a new job.

I rushed up the porch steps and barged open the front door. The house felt ominously quiet, as if no one had been in all day. I hurried through to the kitchen. There was no smell of recently cooked food or any sign of Sage. I dashed down to the basement. Perhaps Zandra was taking a nap. She loved naps. But there was no sign of her.

Could she have stayed late at work? We were busy at animal control. Perhaps a last-minute emergency had come in and she'd been sent out to fix things.

I was about to go back up the basement steps when I noticed a closet door slightly open. I hurried over and discovered it was empty. A quick search of the rest of the basement showed all of Zandra's clothes had gone.

An explosion of panic blasted through me, and my toe beans started sweating. She'd never leave me. We were bonded. I tugged on that bond. It was there but warped. The magic was hinky and felt ready to disintegrate.

This couldn't be happening. I threw out a location spell. There was no sign of Zandra in the whole of Crimson Cove. Had she really left town and not told me where she was going?

I raced back up the basement steps and all the way to the top of the house, looking for Sage. I even tried in the yard where she'd set up a home in the shed, but it was empty.

I desperately needed answers. I'd try Sorcha. She said she was going to the café. She must have an idea of what was going on. Perhaps she knew what job interviews Zandra had gone to.

My witch would be back. Zandra had only packed all her things because she was going away for a few days for interviews and needed plenty of options of clothing to wear to impress her potential new boss.

My hackles lifted, and I hissed to myself. She wouldn't have taken everything just for that. Zandra always traveled light and rarely cared about her appearance.

Before I left the house, I headed back down to the basement. My focus was scattered, and I needed a boost of power. A tiny hit from my magical stones would get me laser targeted and back with Zandra.

I hurried over to where I'd carefully hidden the stones and uncovered them. They were gone.

About the author

K.E. O'Connor (Karen) is the author of the adorably fun Lorna Shadow cozy ghost mystery series, the wickedly funny Crypt Witch paranormal mystery series, the Magical Misfits Mysteries featuring a sassy cat with a bundle of twisty puzzles to solve, the slightly darker Witch Haven paranormal mystery series featuring four troubled witches and their wonderful furry (feathered and web-slinging companions), and the whimsical, delicious Holly Holmes cozy culinary mysteries.

Stay in touch with the fun mysteries:

Newsletter:
www.subscribepage.com/cozymysteries
Website: www.keoconnor.com
Facebook: www.facebook.com/keoconnorauthor

Also by

Witch Haven: Welcome to Witch Haven, where nothing is what it seems. Meet four fabulous witches as they struggle with their destinies, deal with misfiring magic, murder, and the Magic Council.

Crypt Witches: Meet Tempest Crypt, a witch who swallows demons, and Wiggles, her mini talking hellhound, while you enjoy magical murder and intrigue.

Lorna Shadow: A cozy mystery series set in the fun world of a personal assistant who sees ghosts. Meet Lorna, her ditzy sidekick, Helen, and Flipper, the dog who senses ghosts, as they solve crimes and save the day.

Holly Holmes: An adorable cozy culinary mystery series set in the beautiful village of Audley St. Mary. Each book is full of treats, murder, and twists. Join Holly and Meatball, her clue-hunting dog, as they solve murders and eat cake.